I0641297

Damaged

AE Moran

Invisible Publishing Company

Copyright © 2022 by AE Moran

No portion of this book may be reproduced in any form without written permission from the publisher or author, except as permitted by U.S. copyright law.

Contents

Chapter 1: Natalie   1

Chapter 2: Wes   11

Chapter 3: Natalie   17

Chapter 4: Natalie   27

Chapter 5: Wes   35

Chapter 6: Wes   45

Chapter 7: Natalie   51

Chapter 8: Natalie   61

Chapter 9: Wes   69

Chapter 10: Wes   75

Chapter 11: Natalie   81

Chapter 12: Natalie   91

Chapter 13: Natalie   99

Chapter 14: Wes   111

Chapter 15: Wes   121

Chapter 16: Natalie   127

Chapter 17: Wes   139

Chapter 18: Wes   147

Chapter 19: Natalie   153

Chapter 20: Wes   159

Chapter 21: Natalie   163

Chapter 22: Wes   171

Chapter 23: Natalie   179

Chapter 24: Wes   185

Chapter 25: Natalie   193

Chapter 26: Wes   201

Chapter 27: Natalie   207

Chapter 28: Wes   213

Chapter 29: Natalie   219

Chapter 30: Wes   225

Epilogue: Wes   229

Sign Up Once--Get all A.E. Moran's free books includ-   235
ing brand new releases

About AE Moran   237

Also by AE Moran (so far)   239

Chapter 1: Natalie

"Oh, no!" Madelyn Hansen whispers. "Look!"

A prickle runs over my scalp when my team and I turn around to follow Madelyn's gaze. We all stiffen when a group of people approaches the negotiating room entrance—the negotiating room we're about to enter.

"That's Wes Winslow, the CEO of Monarch Resorts Group," Logan Braithwaite murmurs. "What is he doing here?"

"He must be here to negotiate for the sale of the Summit Hotel, the same way we are."

I square my shoulders and turn around to face my team. I draw myself up as best I can and level them with a hard look.

"Now here's what's going to happen. We came here to buy the Summit Hotel. So another group is here to pitch their offer to the hotel owners the same way we are. Who cares? Triple Star Hospitality is the best there is. We'll just have to convince the owners that our offer is the best. That's all there is to it."

"Yeah, but...." Madelyn glances past my shoulder. "You know what they say about Wes Winslow. He plays hardball. If he wants something, he gets it. He won't take any prisoners until he buys the Summit Hotel right out from under us."

"She's right, Natalie," Logan murmurs. "If Wes Winslow is heading this negotiation, we don't stand a chance....and look. He's bringing the whole Monarch executive committee with him. That means Wes will be the one leading this negotiation. We're doomed."

"I don't want to hear that," I tell them. "If Wes Winslow is in the habit of steamrolling people to get what he wants, then we'll just have to be the first people who beat him and teach him a lesson. We'll show him that treating people well is the way to win, not grinding them under your heel. Now come on. We have a hotel to buy."

I turn my back on my team and now I have no choice but to enter the negotiation room. I'm in charge of this team, but I can't help but tremble when I see Wes Winslow in the room waiting for me.

He doesn't see me. He doesn't even know I exist, but he intimidates the hell out of me and we haven't even exchanged a single word yet.

He's a whole lot bigger in person than he looks in pictures. He must be six-foot-five and he's built like a tank with not a scrap of fat anywhere.

His rugged features and short-clipped brown hair give him a granite, chiseled appearance. He looks like a freight train couldn't budge him and his hard grey eyes flick from one thing to another with unerring accuracy.

He wears an immaculately tailored power suit that makes him look even bigger and more imposing. Every detail of his appearance is perfect and flawless down to the last speck of dust. He looks like he's been carved out of marble and just as unfeeling.

He looks just as immovable and determined as his reputation suggests. He leaves a trail of notorious acquisitions in his wake. Anyone would break out in a cold sweat at the thought of entering any negotiation with him, even a friendly one.

Now I'll be standing on the opposite side of the room from him. We'll be competing to see who can convince the Summit Hotel owners to sell us this hotel so the other party can't get it.

Standing out in the hall isn't getting me any closer to accomplishing that. I came here to buy a hotel, not to cower in fear before some guy with a bigger wallet.

I brace myself for the fight of my life and start walking. Wes looks up and his eyes go extra hard and cold when I reach the threshold. He looks right at me and no doubt he can see the rest of my team hiding behind me.

That look tells me loud and clear that he recognizes me as his competition. His executives and my team don't mean anything. This negotiation will come down to him versus me. Whoever wins will take the hotel.

That gives me all the incentive I need to knock this out of the park....and to knock Wes right out of this room. If he's half the cutthroat pirate people say he is, then he needs someone to take him down a peg. He needs someone to teach him that hurting people doesn't pay.

I might not be the best person to teach him that lesson, but I might just have to be.

The Summit Hotel owners obviously planned for Wes and me to face off like this because they've set up the room with three tables arranged in a triangle. The Summit owners occupy one side of the triangle with Wes and his group on the other.

That leaves the last side for me and my team. We move behind our table and Madelyn, Logan, and the others take their seats.

I remain standing. I don't want to let my guard down around Wes. He sits down in his chair and relaxes back like he does this kind of thing all the time. Maybe he does. It wouldn't surprise me.

He starts chatting with the man sitting next to him and the guy laughs, but Wes doesn't even smile. He acts like the Terminator about to blow away everyone in this room. Doesn't the guy have any heart at all?

I become aware that I'm the only person in the room still standing so I sit down, too, but I can't relax.

Fortunately, I don't have to wait long. Ollie Farmer, the patriarch of the Farmer family that owns the Summit Hotel, leans forward and rests his elbows on the table.

His two sons flank him on either side and the two women sitting outside of them are his son's wives. The five of them run the hotel. These are the people I have to convince that Triple Star Hospitality will take better care of their business than Monarch Resorts Group.

Ollie smiles at my team and then at the Monarch group. "Well, thank you all for coming. We can't wait to hear what you have to tell us so let's get started. Representing Triple Star Hospitality, we have Ms. Natalie Fahey and her team. Representing Monarch Resorts Group, we have Mr. Wes Winslow and his executive committee."

I nod across the triangle at Wes and say as politely as I can, "Good to meet you."

He nods back at me. "It's my pleasure."

His flinty, unwavering stare tells me that it definitely won't be a pleasure unless he likes eviscerating nobodies like me. He can be as polite as I can, but once the claws come out, he won't quit until he draws blood.

"Why don't you start us off, Ms. Fahey?" Ollie waves to a screen across the room. "Let us hear what you got."

I walk around the triangle to the computer station by the screen and plug my thumb drive into it. I navigate to my PowerPoint presentation and turn to face the room.

Wes and his fellow executives swivel their chairs backward to face me. I can't help but be painfully aware that Wes is sitting right in front of me. He seems even bigger up close and he makes me feel tiny. He sees everything and never takes his eyes off me.

I take a deep breath and force myself to look at Ollie and his family. They're the only people who count.

"Thank you, Mr. Farmer. Thank you for the opportunity to make you an offer to purchase the Summit Hotel." I launch into my presentation. "The Summit Hotel has a long history as a family enterprise. It was founded by your father, Olsen Farmer, and he, his wife, and you and your three siblings worked in this hotel for decades to build it into the successful enterprise it is today."

I scroll through pictures of Ollie and his family in the hotel's early days. I'm not telling him anything he doesn't already know, but I'm just laying the groundwork for what comes next.

"At Triple Star Hospitality, we pride ourselves on being more than just a hotel chain. Hospitality is the central pillar of our brand and we go out of our way to infuse a culture of family, support, acceptance, and no-holds-barred customer service into every facet of our business. We treat every employee, every guest, and every contractor as a member of one big interconnected family."

I start rolling through pictures of our premises, staff events, and pictures of our people with satisfied guests who have been coming back to us for years.

"Our culture as a close-knit family benefits our bottom line and we have the data to back it up. These charts show the revenue Triple Star was bringing in before we implemented this new cultural shift. The previous Chief Operations Officer had a cutthroat, heartless, take-no-prisoners attitude. He pitted employees against each other and held competitions to see who would win promotion while the loser got fired. Employees who failed to execute difficult projects were unceremoniously fired while the staff was expected to work long hours with no free time for any personal life."

I don't dare to look at Wes. If he doesn't know by now that I'm describing someone just like him, he isn't the man I think he is.

"You can see that when we implemented this culture shift, our profits skyrocketed and our business started thriving as never before. We have more repeat guests now than first-time guests and our customer feedback has been overwhelmingly positive. Our employees take great pride in providing an environment they would offer to their own families and this includes every detail of our premises, our service, and our finances. We have guests intimately involved in the lives of employees and vice versa. We have employees keeping in touch with guests for years after their stay, attending their weddings, visiting their homes, and building strong relationships that last long after the guest leaves our doors. This is the culture the Summit Hotel will be joining if Triple Star Hospitality acquires the hotel. The employees that helped you build this business will become as much a part of our family as they are a part of yours. They won't be left out in the cold and the connection you have with your guests will continue under our banner. Only Triple Star can continue the proud Farmer family tradition you've all worked so hard to build. You won't get this from any other chain. I can promise you that. Thank you for your time and consideration."

"Um....one question, Natalie." Ollie holds up his index finger. I must be the only person in the room that notices him calling me by my first name. The Monarch people don't need to know that I already have a close relationship with Ollie outside of work.

"What can I do for you?" I ask.

"You mentioned that the former Chief Operations Officer used this competitive approach to employee management and that your finances changed when the culture shifted. Are you saying that the culture shifted when you become Chief Operations Officer? Were you the one who implemented this shift?"

"Yes, I was. I worked as an employee at Triple Star before I became an executive. I experienced this competitive culture for myself and I saw firsthand how it affected every guest. It bled into every detail of the guest's stay from the quality of the food to how well the laundry was cleaned. None of the employees felt any pride in their work. None of them had any investment in making the guests' stays a positive experience. The entire business throbbed with hostility and suspicion. It was palpable, so when I became COO, I decided to change it. It took time to convince everyone, but you can see from our bottom line that the effect was dramatic and almost immediate. Now we have employees saying they wouldn't work anywhere else and guests saying they wouldn't stay anywhere else. We can't ask for anything better than that."

I wait for one of the Farmers to ask another question, but when they don't, I go back to my seat and sink into my chair fighting down nerves. I made my pitch. Now it's out of my hands.

Madelyn and Logan both lean in to squeeze my arms. "That was fantastic, Natalie!" Madelyn whispers.

"Congratulations!" Logan breathes. "That was perfect! You're the best, Natalie."

I blush and command myself to relax. My heart is still racing, but I can't help but feel pleased with how well I did. Ollie and his family smile at me from the top table. I did it. I convinced them.

The Farmer family doesn't care about the money. They already have enough of it. They want to know their tradition won't die when they sell the hotel and I gave them that.

Ollie looks away and all eyes turn to the Monarch table. I look over there to find Wes scowling at me. He doesn't look happy at all. In fact, he looks downright dangerous. Did he get offended when I called him cutthroat and heartless?

Whether he got offended doesn't concern me. I hope the Farmer family understands the difference between our two businesses. Then they'll realize they don't want their beloved hotel going to a blood-thirsty cannibal like Wes Winslow.

"Well, Mr. Winslow?" Ollie prompts. "We're all ears. You're going to have a tall order following that act."

Wes stands up....and up....and up. Man, he's tall! I haven't seen a guy that big in a long time. He really strikes an imposing figure—unlike me—but when he takes his place at the screen and faces the room, a noticeable chill falls over the people sitting in front of him.

A subtle grip of fear seizes my heart when I see how hard and impenetrable he looks. He embodies every negative quality I just described. He's cold, ruthless, and he doesn't care about the human aspect of the hospitality industry.

He looks like the kind of guy that would make his employees compete for promotion with the loser getting thrown out on the sidewalk. He radiates that aura of callous disregard for anything beyond his bottom line.

He launches into his pitch and I get another thrill of triumph when he starts describing how successful Monarch Resorts Group is. He describes in detail how much profit they earn, how much they allocate to improvements and development, their stock share price, and he goes through a comparison of their room prices against similar rooms offered by their competition.

My hackles rise when he uses some examples from Triple Star properties, but my heart leaps again when I realize that our rooms and amenities are just as good as Monarch's but we're offering them at a lower rate.

He goes on at length, but he never mentions Monarch's company culture. He never even touches on anything related to Monarch's commitment to hospitality. He doesn't say the word 'hospitality' once in his whole pitch.

My blood pumps faster as he reaches the end of his presentation. Ollie and his family listen intently, but I don't see any of them smiling. I did it. I won.

Wes made my case for me even better than I could have. The Farmer family can see that Wes doesn't give a damn about their tradition or their people or the guests who have been coming back to them for years. He only cares about the money. I got this hotel in the bag.

Chapter 2: Wes

I stand up from the negotiating table and lean my hands on the edge while I get my head together. I can't believe that negotiation went as badly as it did.

Jim Kaufman, my CFO, says something in my ear, but I barely hear him. I came to this negotiation expecting to go home with the Summit Hotel in my back pocket. How did it all turn against me?

I only have to look across the room to get the answer. That woman stands with her team and I can see the opposite written all over her face. She beams in triumph, hugs her friends, and they laugh delightedly. They know they won. She won.

How did she beat me so easily? I still don't understand it, but I know it's true when Ollie Farmer and his sons go over to the Triple Star Hospitality group. The Farmers hug her and shake hands with the rest of her team. The Farmers don't come over to me.

Natalie. Natalie Fahey. I've never seen her before, but I'm going straight back to the office to find out everything I can about her.

She's the Chief Operations Officer for Triple Star Hospitality. Triple Star is Monarch Resorts Groups' competition, but Triple Star doesn't operate the luxury resorts and high-end hotels that Monarch prides itself on.

That must be how she slipped under my radar. I underestimated Triple Star because we cater to different clientele, but that was obviously a mistake. I need to change that quickly. I can't let anything like this happen again.

I make a point not to stare at her across the room, but everything about her remains etched into my memory.

I don't need to look at her because I will never, ever be able to forget her. I'll keep playing her pitch over and over in my mind for the rest of my life and that means I'll keep seeing *her* in my mind, too.

She's so tiny. She can't be more than five-foot-five with a tight, athletic build that makes me feel huge by comparison. My size usually helps me in the business world. Now it just makes me feel clumsy. I'm missing some crucial piece of the puzzle here and I don't even know what it is.

She wears her wavy brown hair drawn back in a half ponytail with long draping coils framing her petite little face. Her delicate features and bright black eyes give her a fragile, almost childlike look, but she moves gracefully and her musical voice carries across the room.

She wears a classy business suit with a gold chain tucked under her shirt collar and very nice high heels beneath her knee-length skirt. Everything about her looks put-together, but that tells me nothing about how effectively she handled that negotiation.

A woman like that shouldn't intimidate me, but she does. I don't know how to deal with her. She's my competition and she obviously knows how to throw her influence around. I want to fight her, but I won't be able to beat her that way.

I start to gather up my stuff when Ollie finally comes over to me. He shakes my hand, but he doesn't even try to hug me. I can't imagine hugging someone whose business I'm trying to acquire. That's what

I don't understand about her. She acts so unprofessionally, but her methods are clearly more effective than mine. I don't get it at all.

"Thank you for coming in, Mr. Winslow," Ollie tells me.

"Thank you for having me. It was a pleasure."

He doesn't call me by my first name. I can't help but rankle that he called Natalie by her first name. He did it in the middle of her pitch which means he slipped up. He must be in the habit of calling her that and he didn't stop himself in time.

He would never make a mistake like that with me. I can't remember one time in my whole business career when I wanted someone to call me by my first name. I would have considered that a sign of disrespect, but she doesn't.

"Come next door and have lunch with us," Ollie tells me. "We can leave our boxing gloves in here."

He laughs, but I can't join in. Everything that happened today throws my world into turmoil. These people are speaking a language I don't understand, but she understands it no question.

My group files out of the room. They get mixed up with Natalie, her team, and the Farmer family. Everyone talks and several of them laugh. They look happy and relieved now that the negotiation is over, but I'm not. I want to go back in there and duke it out with her, but it's too late for that.

I have no choice but to go into the next room where a bunch of nibbles lie out on a buffet table. Natalie, her team, and the Farmers are all already in there talking and laughing like they've known each other for years. Maybe they have. I don't know.

Even some Monarch executives go over to talk to her and congratulate her on her pitch. She draws them into her circle and starts talking to them like she's known them for years, too.

I bristle that my own people are cozying up to the enemy, but she isn't the enemy anymore. We both made our pitches. Now it's up to the Farmer family to decide who they want to sell their hotel to. I don't really have to wonder.

I go over to the buffet table. I don't feel like eating so I get a bottle of water. A few of my execs come over and talk to me about business. I answer them and we shoot a few ideas back and forth, but I keep an eye on Natalie.

I would be very surprised if she's over there talking business with her team. They keep laughing and she blushes when one guy nudges her with his elbow. Are they involved? Could she really be that unprofessional that she would get involved with one of her employees?

I don't know anything about her and I realize with a wince that I don't really know much about Triple Star Hospitality, either. Everything she said about their culture was news to me. I didn't know they had a culture at all.

I knew her predecessor—the man she claimed made his employees compete for promotion. Bill Simons was a good businessman. He knew how to get good work out of his people. I have a hard time reconciling her description with the man I knew.

I don't know about her claim that he fostered an atmosphere of hostility and suspicion, but if she worked under him as an employee, she must have experienced it for herself.

And then there are the charts she showed. How could a simple shift in company culture cause such a massive change in profits? I'm going to have to investigate this, but since I've never encountered this in more than fifteen years in business, I don't even know where to look.

Luckily for me, I have a resource right in front of me. I wait for a break in the conversation, and when two of Natalie's people move over to the buffet table, I take my chance.

I walk across the room toward her and the crowd parts to let me through. I've always prided myself on having that effect on people. They always move out of my way when I go anywhere, but now I notice a definite chill fall over the room as I approach Natalie. People shrink away like I might be dangerous or something.

I like that people think I'm dangerous. I want them to think that—or I did want it before today. Now it strikes me as all wrong.

She stiffens and the conversation dies when I stop in front of her. "Congratulations, Ms. Fahey. That was a great pitch. You obviously understand your audience."

She stares at me in what I can only imagine is petrified horror and then, amazingly, she bursts out laughing. "You don't have to call me that. Call me Natalie. Everyone does."

A woman on her team laughs, too. "When was the last time anyone at Triple Star called you 'Ms. Fahey'?"

The woman lays extra emphasis on the last two words and the whole group laughs like calling her Ms. Fahey is a big joke. Natalie blushes again. "It makes me sound like a school marm."

She gets another laugh out of them. Don't ask me why. I have no idea why they find this so funny.

She turns back to me. "Can I ask you a question, Mr. Winslow?"

Her saying my name sounds wrong. She just told me to call her by her first name, so now I have to do the same thing. "Call me Wes."

"Did you know we were going to be here today?" she asks. "Did you know you were going to be negotiating against Triple Star?"

"Yes, I knew. Ollie told me when he invited me to come in and make a counter-pitch. Why do you ask?"

"Why did you use Triple Star properties in your comparison?" she asks. "I would have thought you'd avoid comparing Monarch with Triple Star."

"Why would I avoid it? You're our competition and you're offering comparable amenities. I wanted to show that we charge more for the same offering. Why do you ask?"

"I'm just curious because the Summit Hotel promotes itself as a value offering. It doesn't promote itself as luxury or exclusive or elite."

I stare at her feeling sick to my stomach. She's right. I targeted my pitch to try to flatter the Farmers. I wanted them to think we considered the Summit Hotel good enough to join our chain.

I should have done more research on their offering. Of course the hotel's current customer base won't be interested in anything luxury or exclusive or elite if they've been coming to the Summit Hotel for value. I should have thought of that. Now I probably missed out on buying this hotel.

I take a step forward. "I'd like to talk to you, Ms. Fahey. I'd like to discuss your methods of running operations at Triple Star. I'd like to figure out how I can harness your unique talents to benefit Monarch."

She snorts very softly through her nose. "I already have a job, Mr. Winslow. I'm not looking for another one."

She walks off and a few of her team members give me dirty looks when they follow her away. She goes over to Ollie and hugs him again. Then she hugs all four of his family members before she leaves.

How does she do it? How does she get everyone to love her like this? I don't see her doing anything except breaking the boundaries of professionalism, but she has a way of winning everyone over. It's the opposite of everything I know about business.

Chapter 3: Natalie

I walk into the laundry room in the deepest bowels of the Celestial Hotel. The hotel covers the bottom half of our downtown skyscraper with the Triple Star Hospitality corporate headquarters filling the top half of the building.

I hit a massive wall of steam before I push through it to the laundry room. A dozen huge, sweaty ex-convicts work down here, each one twice my size.

Big Baner spots me first. He's an enormous, muscle-bound, black, bald, former gangbanger with a million tattoos and a mouthful of gold teeth. "Hey! It's my main girl!" He throws out both arms and struts across the room to swallow me in a giant hug. "You coming down to fold the laundry with us, baby? You can't keep away from me, can you?"

I laugh and hug him back. "You know the ladies can't resist you, Baner."

He explodes in raucous laughter and the rest of the guys join in. They start yelling jokes and insults across the room while they work.

I turn to the hulking hydraulic press in the corner. "Why hasn't maintenance come down here to fix this yet?"

"Mitch from Property said they're too busy fitting out the North Star site," Baner tells me. "He said he won't be able to send anyone for at least a week."

"We can't wait that long," I reply. "We need the press working before that. I'll straighten him out."

"You straighten him out, boss!" one of the other guys yells out. "Stretch him on the rack and step on him in your high heels. Make him beg for mercy!"

They all laugh again and I join in, but when I take out my phone to call the maintenance manager about fixing the press, the phone rings in my hand.

I press it to my ear. "Natalie Fahey speaking."

"Nat! It's me! It's Gina Watts from reception." She whispers in a rushed undertone so I can barely hear her.

"Gina! What's up? Is everything all right?" It can't be if she's calling me. Most of my employees love their work. They only call me if something's wrong.

"You HAVE to get to reception right away!" she breathes. "It's an emergency!"

"What's going on? I'm on my way upstairs right now. Do we need to call 911?"

"I can't explain it to you over the phone." She whispers even lower. She sounds like she has her hand over the speaker. "You'll understand when you get here."

She hangs up and I stare at the phone. What the hell is that about?

I wave to the laundry guys and ride the elevator up to the ground floor. I expect to find the place on fire or maybe inundated by a tsunami or something, but everything looks in order.

I walk over to the reception desk and my world comes to a screeching halt when I see Wes Winslow standing by the desk. Gina cowers in front of him trying to work in between shooting him petrified glances over her glasses.

I can also see a few guests milling around in the foyer entrance. None of them want to go near the desk with Wes there. He casts a cloud of intimidation wherever he goes. I can't let this continue.

Gina nearly breaks down crying in relief when I walk over to confront Wes. His eyes go hard when he sees me and then they flick down to my clothes.

I'm not wearing a power suit like I was at the negotiation. I always wear business casual at work. Today, I'm wearing khaki capri pants, flat white sneakers, and a beige blazer over a white t-shirt.

I don't know what he was expecting, but it definitely wasn't this. Maybe he thought I went around in a power suit all the time. That's what he's wearing so that explains why he thinks everyone should be like him.

"What can I do for you, Mr. Winslow?" I ask.

"I'd like to talk to you about the Summit negotiation."

"What is there to talk about? We negotiated. We made our pitches. What the owners do with those pitches is out of our hands."

"I know that. I don't want to talk about our pitches."

"Please tell me you didn't come over here to try to convince me to withdraw Triple Star's offer. Whatever it is you're pushing, I'm not interested."

"I didn't come here for that and I'm not pushing anything. I want to talk to you."

He towers over me just as brooding and impervious as ever. If he's angry that I beat him at the negotiating table, he has a strange way of showing it.

I glance over at Gina and she gives me a pleading look. None of the guests have worked up the courage to approach the desk yet. I really have to end this conversation now, but I also need to make sure he doesn't come back here causing another disturbance.

"Come over here, please." I motion for him to follow me into the nearest lounge. If he was anyone else, I would have touched his arm, but I can't do that with him.

I'm not afraid to touch him. I'm not afraid of him at all. He isn't that much bigger than Baner and Baner always hugs me and even kisses me on the head whenever we see each other.

I can't do that with Wes. Something in the iron façade of his bulk and radiating power stops me. He wouldn't appreciate an intimate gesture like touching his arm.

I don't understand his need to intimidate everyone with his smoldering personality and volcanic presence, but maybe I'm wrong about that, too. Maybe he doesn't even realize he's doing it. Maybe it just comes naturally to him.

I get him out of the line of sight from the reception desk before I confront him again. I have to look almost straight up to maintain eye contact with him, but he doesn't scare me. Something about him makes me curious to find out how he ticks. That's just what comes naturally to me.

"What did you want to talk to me about?" I ask.

"I want to talk to you about your pitch."

I compress my lips and resist the urge to smack them in annoyance. "I already told you I won't withdraw our offer...."

"I'm not talking about your offer. I'm talking about everything you said about your company culture and how you changed it to improve your bottom line."

"If you were listening to my pitch at all, you would have heard that I didn't change it to improve our bottom line. I changed it to improve the atmosphere of our business to one of cooperation and mutual support. I did it to improve working conditions for our employees, to improve the environment for our guests, and to make Triple Star a place where people would want to come and not avoid. The improvement to our bottom line came after that."

"That's exactly what I want to talk to you about. I want to talk to you about how you did it, why you did it, and all the consequences afterward."

I frown up at him. "Why do you want to know all that?"

"Call it professional curiosity. I want to consult with you in a professional capacity so I can improve our workings at Monarch."

Now I don't even try to stop myself from smacking my lips. "I already told you I'm not interested in helping Monarch. I'm not interested in anything that happens at Monarch. We're finished here, Mr. Winslow. Have a nice day."

"Then do it on a personal basis—not for Monarch. Do it to satisfy my curiosity." He waves toward the lounge where people sit around watching us. "If one of these people asked you to explain your business to them, would you do it?"

I follow his gesture and realize that he's right. If any random person asked me how I changed Triple Star's culture, I wouldn't hesitate to explain it at length. It's only him that makes me question.

I don't want to let my guard down around him in case he tries to trap me. Maybe this is a trick to get the Summit Hotel after all.

I study him more closely. He has a fearsome reputation, but he's also widely respected as a consummate professional. He doesn't pull dirty tricks. He accomplishes everything by being the best at everything. He covers all his bases—except for the cultural and personal touch aspects of it.

That must be why he's asking. He wants to improve. I can respect that.

"All right," I agree. "What do you want to know that I haven't already explained?"

"Do you mind if we sit down somewhere?" He glances behind me. "It's eleven-thirty. Have lunch with me in your restaurant over there and we can talk while we eat."

I hesitate again. Having lunch with him is the absolute last thing in the world I want to do. I can think of hundreds or even thousands of people I'd rather have lunch with, but if he's serious, we can't exactly discuss business standing up. This could take a while.

"All right," I say again. "I'll give you half an hour. It's time for my lunch break anyway."

We go over to the restaurant and I see people turning to watch us pass. Their heads swivel taking in the sight. He's so much bigger than I am. We look like cartoon characters walking side by side.

I smile at several people including employees who give me petrified looks when they see me with the Dreaded Monster. Some of them have come to work for Triple Star after leaving Monarch. They know who he is and they're all terrified of him.

I step into the restaurant and take in the scene in one glance. I know almost everyone in here and they're all surprised to see me. I never eat in here, but I'm always down here doing something or other, checking in with the employees, going over the ordering with the head chef, and all the other business of running the hotel.

Sergio, the concierge, is seating a couple at their table. His podium at the front stands empty so Wes and I stop there to wait for Sergio to come back. One of the waitresses is clearing a nearby table and turns around to smile at me. "Hi, Natalie. What brings you down here?"

"Just getting lunch, Charlotte. How's the new baby? Is he sleeping yet?"

Charlotte glances left and right and lowers her voice to a conspiratorial whisper. "Don't tell anyone, but Martin took the baby for a three-hour drive around the airport parking lot on Saturday. I couldn't take it anymore, so Martin just kept driving around and around and around while the baby got a decent nap for a change. It was heaven!"

We both laugh and she takes off into the back. She looks more cheerful now that we've talked. One of Sergio's diners is having a problem. He's taking extra long to get back here. I need to ask him about that.

One of the busboys comes over to wipe down Charlotte's table. He carries a plastic tub in his arms and sets it on the table while he talks to me over his shoulder. "Would you and your date like something to drink, Natalie?"

I take a second to realize he's talking about Wes. I open my mouth to explain why Wes is here, but I change my mind. It would take too long to explain.

"I'm good, Tommy. Thank you. I'll get a drink from Charlotte. How are you? Did you get your car fixed?"

He breaks into a grin. "I asked my dad about it and he said...."

He picks up his tub and turns around to face me. At that moment, another diner who was walking out of the restaurant suddenly spins around, takes off in the opposite direction, and collides full tilt with Tommy's tub.

The tub hits the floor and all the used glasses and plates in it smash across the carpet along with ice, spilled drinks, and uneaten potato salad.

The diner springs back in horror. He was fiddling with his phone and not looking where he was going. "Oh, my God! I am so sorry! It's all my fault! I'll pay for it! I'm sorry!" He rushes Tommy and grabs Tommy's shoulder. "Are you all right? Oh, my God! I am so sorry!"

"It's all right," Tommy tells him. "No big deal."

He bends down and starts putting all the broken glass and shattered crockery back in the tub before wiping up the food and spilled drinks with his rag.

I kneel next to him and help him out. "Don't worry about it, Sir. It was an accident."

"No, really! I want to pay for it. I am so sorry, young man! I'm so careless. Are you hurt?"

"I'm fine." Tommy shoots me a small smile and then smiles broadly at the man. "Really. You don't have to worry about it."

The guy looks stricken that we won't let him pay for it. Tommy and I finish picking everything up. He cleans the carpet as well as he can, mumbles, "Thanks," to me, and hurries away.

I turn to the man who is practically in tears. "I am so sorry!" he wails. "I'm so careless."

"It's okay." I pat him on the shoulder. "It happens to the best of us. Really. Go on. You don't have to hang around here apologizing anymore."

He pinches his lips, squeaks out one last, "Thank you!" and leaves.

I turn back to Wes, who stands there watching the whole incident. He doesn't move or offer a word of input, and just then, Sergio comes back. "Sorry about that, Nat. What can I do for you?"

"We're here for lunch. What was that delay about, Sergio? Are those people okay?"

"The old lady is stone deaf. She couldn't hear a word I said. I had to repeat everything four times." He laughs. "They're all right now." His face falls when he sees Wes. "Are you......?"

"This is Wes Winslow from Monarch Resorts Group. We're here for a business lunch. Do you have any tables that aren't reserved?"

"Sure. Follow me."

He takes us to a table for two in the corner, shoots Wes one more wary glance, and hands us our menus. "Charlotte will be your server. Let me know if you need anything at all."

Chapter 4:
Natalie

Wes and I face each other across the restaurant table. I don't know what to say to him. If he can't see how everyone at Triple Star treats each other, I don't know how else to explain it to him.

"Explain your approach to operations," he begins. "What's your methodology?"

"Methodology!" I repeat. "I don't have a methodology except to treat everyone like family. I told you that. You can see for yourself how it is here."

"I can see how it is here, but I still want to understand how you approach it. I did some research on Triple Star and the differences you pointed out between when Bill Simons ran the company and after you took over."

I stiffen at that name. "Bill Simons was a tyrant and a sadist. He was the worst boss any employee could wind up with. I made a promise to myself when I worked under him that I would change things if I ever got a chance and that's what I did."

"How did you do it? What did you do first?"

"First, I called a meeting of the Board of Directors and the executive. I pointed out that our numbers were suffering because we had so few repeat guests and such high staff turnover."

"Ah!" he exclaims. "So it did start with the bottom line."

"No, it didn't. I only told them that so they would see how it impacted our business. I explained that Bill made working conditions intolerable for everyone under him and that was creating a hostile atmosphere for the guests. Our reviews were terrible and too many guests were saying they would never stay with us again if you paid them to do it."

"What did you do after you informed the board and the executive?"

"I called all the managers and explained what I wanted to do. Then I sent out invitations to company barbecues where all the staff could socialize and get to know each other outside of work."

He frowns. "What did you do that for?"

"I just told you—so we could socialize and get to know each other outside of work. I told everyone I wanted to change the culture and what I wanted to change it to. I held a bunch of events on the company time clock where the staff could just kick back, relax, and engage as a family with no pressure to perform."

He won't stop frowning at me. "Um.... okay. And did that work?"

"It worked great—that and changing our hiring process. Now I explain the company culture to all our new hires. It's easier now because they get integrated into the family culture as soon as they start working here, but at the beginning, it took a little longer."

"So how did you overcome their resistance to the change?"

I shrug. "I just walked around talking to people, making sure they were all right, giving them whatever support they needed—that kind of thing—kind of like I do now. It was the same then and it just spread. It spread to the whole company."

He sits there frowning at me for another minute until Charlotte comes over to take our order. I get a large Cobb salad. Wes gets a steak with all the trimmings. I guess he needs to eat a lot to fuel that big body of his.

He looks like he works out a lot. I notice it more now that I'm sitting in front of him. The veins on his hands and wrists stand out from his skin. His shirt buttons strain across the expanse of muscle that is his chest.

Charlotte places glasses of water in front of both of us. "Can I get you anything to drink, Nat—Sir?" Her expression completely changes when she looks at Wes.

"I don't need anything. Thanks, Charlotte," I reply.

"I don't want anything, either," Wes replies. "I never drink anything but water."

Charlotte gives me a surprised look and then leaves. "Why don't you drink anything but water?" I ask.

"I don't consume any liquid calories," he tells me. "I'm on a strict diet and liquid calories are out. My mental acuity suffers if I don't eat the right foods at the right times."

"Wow," I exclaim. "I had no idea you were such a well-oiled machine."

His eyebrows come together for a split second before he blows off my comment. Maybe he's used to people calling him a machine. How should I know? He sure acts like one.

"Anyway, getting back to the subject of your methodology...."

"I already told you I don't have a methodology. I just treat everyone like family and they treat me like family. That's all there is to it. There is no secret science behind it. You're overthinking this way too much."

"What exactly does that mean to you? What do you mean by treating everyone like family?"

I open my mouth to say something and stop. "What do you mean?"

"What does 'treating everyone like family' mean? Break it down for me."

I hesitate again. "I don't get what you're asking. It's obvious, isn't it? You're running a hospitality business. Surely even you must understand the need to treat people well."

"There's a difference between treating people well and what you're doing. I checked your reviews and your records. Your track record of customer service, guest satisfaction, and employee retention is unrivaled in the whole industry and it's consistent across your entire chain—not just here in the hotel where you work. It's everywhere across hundreds of locations."

"That's what I've been telling you. People want to stay here because they feel at home here. That goes for guests and employees alike. What's so hard to understand about that?"

"This is exactly what I want to learn from you," he replies.

"How could you possibly learn it from me when you already know what you need to do? If I had to guess, I'd say you don't really want to change it at all. You're just more interested in your bottom line than you are in people's experiences when they come into contact with your business. You could change it if you really wanted to. What is there to stop you?"

"I don't know how to. You keep talking about treating everyone like family, but I don't know what that means."

"How can you not know what it means? You have a family. Just treat people the same way you would treat your mother or your father or your sister or your brother. It's basic human relations."

"I don't have a family. I have never had one. That's why I'm asking. I don't have a frame of reference for it."

I open my mouth one more time, but I can't make a sound. Did he just say what I thought he said?

"I was placed in foster care when I was a year and a half old," he tells me. "I grew up in the system and I started my own business when I was fifteen. I've never had a family or any long-term relationships. My longest relationship was seven months and it didn't go anywhere. I don't really understand what family is."

I swallow hard and barely notice when Charlotte shows up with our food. I can't believe I'm sitting across the table from someone who has never had a family—ever.

I can't imagine a more nightmarish existence than that. He must be about thirty now and he's been living alone all that time. No wonder he's so wooden.

My heart twists thinking about him as a child. He never had a mother or a father to care about him. No one ever put him to bed or wiped away his tears. No one supported him in his ambitions. He's gone through all of that alone. My God, what a nightmare!

"Are you okay?" he asks. "Did I say something to offend you?"

I bend over my salad and stab my fork into it. I take a bite while I try to decide what to say to him. I can't get over the heartbreak of what he's describing. That explains why he finds this culture at Triple Star so foreign.

It also explains why he didn't think to address the family tradition at the Summit Hotel. He doesn't realize how important it is or what he's missing out on. He doesn't even see how heartbreaking his situation is.

"Would you like me to leave?" he asks. "I apologize if I made you uncomfortable. I thought you wanted me to explain why I didn't understand what you were saying."

"It's.... it's okay." I flounder to get my voice working.

I can't help seeing Sergio and Charlotte and Tommy and all the other employees working in the restaurant. They all have families outside of Triple Star. That's why they're here. Triple Star makes them feel at home.

Wes is the only one standing on the outside. He's the only one who doesn't belong here.

"I understand if you don't want to do it, but I'd like to shadow you around for a while," he goes on. "I'd like to observe how you run your business so I can begin to understand the difference between Triple Star and Monarch. I realize you don't want to help out your competition, but I'd be willing to pay you a consulting fee if that makes any difference."

"No...." I stammer. "You don't have to do that. You can shadow me. I......"

I don't finish. I need to do something about this. There has to be a way to help him. At least he realizes that something is missing. That's why he's here. He needs my help and he's asking for it.

"So?" he prompts. "Do you think you can explain it to me, now that you understand my question?"

"Yeah, I guess so. I guess treating people like family means that you treat their concerns and challenges and struggles as just as important as your own. You treat them in such a way that you acknowledge how their challenges and struggles impact you. You want to help them and solve their problems because those problems are just as big a problem for you as they are for the other person."

"How do their challenges and struggles impact me?"

"Apart from the obvious impact that they have on your business, you mean?"

"How would their challenges and struggles impact my business? They come to us for a place to sleep, not to have their problems solved. That's their job, not ours."

"That's where you're wrong," I tell him. "If an old person who can hardly walk comes to you as a guest, it follows that their challenges are your problem because you have to accommodate their disability. You make their stay as frictionless as possible, and when they see you taking a personal interest in making them comfortable and their stay easy and effortless, they decide to come back because they appreciate the extra effort you put into it. If you have a family with small children come to stay and you go out of your way to make sure the kids have somewhere to play safely so their parents can relax without worry, then the parents decide to come back. They leave a positive review so other parents decide to come and stay with you. It's basic business logic."

He shrugs. "I guess so."

"Don't tell me you never thought of any of this before."

"Not really. We're more concerned with creating an aesthetically appealing environment that people enjoy coming to. Our guests want luxury, beauty, and status. They don't care so much for all those personal touches."

"You're wrong. I bet if Triple Star took over one of your hotels, we would find a way to make their stay so much better by adding those touches. You should try it."

"Anyway," he goes on. "Would you mind if I shadow you today? Would that inconvenience you?"

"Not really. You can if you want to."

"So what did you mean about the impact other people's challenges would have apart from business?" he asks.

"Well, there's the obvious human impact."

"What human impact?"

"The impact of someone suffering and struggling in a way where you have the means and the ability to lighten their burden. Being around someone who is suffering and struggling makes you want to help them as a human being. It's a fundamental drive of human nature to want to relieve suffering and make people happy."

He doesn't say anything while he saws a corner off his steak, puts it in his mouth, and chews it. I can't tell if he understood a word I just said.

He really is like no one I've ever met. Is he even capable of feeling anything for anyone?

Chapter 5: Wes

I walk at Natalie's side on our way through the Celestial Hotel. It takes a lot longer than it should because all the employees and most of the guests stop to talk to her.

I get shunted to the side every time this happens. It annoys me at first, but after about the tenth or eleventh time it happens, I realize that this is what she's showing me.

She knows all of her staff by name. She knows their intimate personal details and every problem each of them is facing at the moment. A few of them even burst into tears and cry on her shoulder. She either comforts them, or in some cases, promises to look into it or do something about it.

We head for the elevator when one of the maids comes over to Natalie. It's obvious this woman doesn't belong on the main floor. She's specifically come over here to seek Natalie out.

Natalie hugs her, and as soon as the maid leaves, she turns back to me. "Do you see how it is? These are my people. No one in the world is more important to me than these people. Everything that affects them affects me. It hurts me when they're hurting and it makes me happy when they're doing well. That's what being family means."

"I see that you're doing it. I just don't know how I would do it."

She turns away to push the elevator button. "Right. That's where it's going to get tricky."

"What do you mean when you say no one in the world is more important to you than these people? Don't you have a family of your own?"

"I have a family." She doesn't look at me when she says it. She steps into the elevator and faces front like I'm not there.

"Where are they?" I ask. "Why aren't you as intimately involved with them as you are with these people?"

"I'm intimately involved with the members of my family who want to be intimately involved with me. My dad and my older sister live in Ontario. I talk to them every other day and visit them three times a year. We're close. My mom and my two brothers live in Arizona and we aren't close. They don't want that kind of closeness with me."

"Why not?"

"I'm not sure. They won't tell me."

I frown at the side of her face. She keeps her features blank and she talks in a dull, emotionless undertone. She completely buries all her vivacious energy that was so obvious just a minute ago.

"Anyway, I've tried several times and I can't get through to them so I just gave up after a while. Now I have those close relationships with my dad and my sister....and these people here. They're my family."

"I'm sorry to hear that," I tell her.

She snaps back to life and smiles up at me. "At least I have one. I feel sorry for you."

"Is that why you're helping me—because you feel sorry for me?"

"Something like that. Let's just say that, if any random person came into my hotel and told me they had a problem that they needed help solving, I would do anything to help them solve it. That's basically what you're doing, isn't it?"

"I guess so." Now it's my turn to face front. I don't like her saying she feels sorry for me, but she's right. I did come here to get her help to solve my problem. Just don't ask me how she's going to solve it. "I guess it's hard for me to think I have a problem at all. I don't think of it as a problem."

"It's a problem if it's affecting your business. It's a problem if I took the Summit Hotel away from you. Is that enough of a problem for you to realize you need to solve it?"

"You're right. It is."

She laughs and her whole face lights up. She understands me pretty well considering this is only our second conversation.

The elevator dings and we step out into a corporate office. Cubicles fill a large section of floor with larger offices surrounding that.

She goes down another long corridor lined with even bigger offices and finally enters a large, comfortable office set into the corner of the building. Windows on two walls look out at a grand view of the city. This must be her office.

"Don't worry. We won't stay up here," she tells me. "I'm going downstairs to interview a new hire so you can come with me and see how I do it. You can take a seat while you wait."

She waves me toward a sectional couch in the corner. I sit down while she messes around on her desk, but she leaves it a minute later.

We get back in the elevator and go down to the ground floor again. This time, she goes to the maintenance department in the back of the building, but she has exactly the same problem no matter where she goes. Everyone constantly comes over to her to talk, to greet her, or to pour out their troubles.

She never tries to push anyone away. She never implies by word or deed that where she's going is more important than whatever it is they want to talk to her about.

She finally throws open the door to a massive workshop full of men in overalls working on various pieces of equipment.

She goes into the manager's office. "Mitch!" she yells over the noise coming from the main floor. "I need you to go downstairs and fix the laundry press. I need it done by the end of the day."

"Can't do that, Nat," he tells her. "All my guys are over at the North Star site."

"And yet here you are sitting behind your desk," she counters. "If you can't spare any of your guys, go down there and fix it yourself."

"Aw, Nat!" he groans. "I can't do that."

"If you don't fix it, the Celestial will shut down and we'll all be in trouble. The press is more important than the North Star. Go on. Go fix it now and get it over with."

He grumbles a lot, but he eventually leaves her alone in his office. "So where's the new hire?" I ask.

"He's meeting us here." She checks her watch. "He has five minutes before he's supposed to get...."

She breaks off when a scrawny kid slouches in. He can't be more than twenty, but he looks much younger.

He keeps his eyes down on the floor when he pulls up in front of her. "Hi, Petey," she greets him in her cheeriest tone. "Thank you for coming in."

"Yes, Ma'am," he mumbles. "Thank you for taking the time to talk to me."

"You don't have to call me that, Petey. Call me Natalie. Everyone around here does."

"Yes, Ma'am."

The slightest trace of a smile tugs at her lips, but he doesn't see. "You answered our ad for someone to work in the hotel laundry. I hear you know Morland James who also works down there."

"Yes, Ma'am." His eyes dart sideways, but he doesn't look up. He keeps mumbling under his breath. "We met...in prison. He got out a year before me. I just got out last month, but no one will hire me because I have a record."

"I know you just got out of prison, Petey. I talked to your parole officer three days ago."

He forgets himself and looks up suddenly. "You did?"

"He told me you worked in the prison laundry for three years before you got out and he says your behavior was exemplary the whole time you were inside. He also told me that you specifically requested a transfer to another unit so you wouldn't be with the guys you got arrested with. He said you've been taking online classes to get your high school diploma and you've been attending the Poetry Slam every Friday since you got out. Stop me if I'm getting any of this wrong."

He stares at her and then looks down at the floor again. "Yes, Ma'am. That's all correct."

"We have a culture of family at Triple Star Hospitality, Petey. Everyone who works here treats each other as family and we treat our guests as family. We expect everyone who comes to work here to honor that and for you to treat all your co-workers with the same respect and goodwill you'd give your mother or your brother. Do you understand?"

"Yes, Ma'am."

"We also expect you to treat the guests as family. We expect you to wash every piece of laundry as if you were getting ready for your mother to come and stay at your house. If you ever deal with any guest, we expect you to talk to them, help them out, and take care of them as if they were the most important person in your life. Do you think you can do that?"

"Yes, Ma'am."

"If you have any problems or difficulties in your life, if you have any trouble adjusting to life on the outside, you can come to me or to any of your co-workers and we'll do anything we can to help you. That's what we're here for—to support you and help you out with anything you need."

He doesn't answer at all. His eyes keep skipping from side to side while he decides whether to believe her.

"Well, the job is yours if you want it. We'd be happy to have you."

He looks up just as surprised. "You would?"

"Yeah. Why don't you come downstairs with us and I'll introduce you to the guys? They're all ex-cons so you should feel right at home."

His head snaps up again. "They are?"

"Yeah!" She beams at him and claps him on the shoulder. "Come on. I'll show you."

We go back outside and I drop back so he can walk next to her. "Morland tells me that you two met in the basic reading program inside. He says you were really great at helping him learn how to read. That's exactly the kind of person we want working at Triple Star."

"Ma'am...." he stammers. "You don't care that.... I'm an ex-con?"

"We only care about how you act once you start working here. You've already shown a strong work ethic and a desire to turn your life around. That's all we care about. We're here to support you and help you make that happen. All the guys downstairs are taking classes doing something or other. None of them want to spend the rest of their lives folding laundry and that's just fine with us. Last year, we had a former employee come in and talk to the guys. He served fifteen years for armed robbery, worked for Triple Star for five years, and now he works for the state legislature."

Petey snaps around to gape at her, but she only smiles at him before she escorts him and me back into the elevator.

We ride down to the basement while she keeps filling his head full of the success stories her approach to human resources has had with people just like him.

We step out into a brightly lit room full of huge, tattooed, ugly, grizzled guys who look like they're still in prison except that they all talk and laugh easily.

A massive black dude with all gold teeth drops what he's doing and spreads his arms coming toward Natalie. "My baby! Who's my best girl?"

He drowns her in a giant hug and she laughs. "I just can't get enough of you, Baner."

"Hey! What about me, Nat?" a bearded Hell's Angels type calls out. "Give your boy Rocker some love!"

She tears herself away from Baner and hugs Rocker, too. Then it's all on as she goes around the room hugging every one of them and in some cases kissing them on their cheeks or foreheads or any other part of them she can reach. She doesn't kiss any of them on the mouth, though, but none of them seems too interested in that.

I can't help but remark on how much everyone loves her. These guys are just much more demonstrative about it than anyone upstairs.

"I brought you a new guy," she tells them. "This is Petey. He just got out a month ago."

Rocker waves to him. "Howdy, bud. You came to the right place."

Natalie points out everyone in the room. "That over there is Fernando Chavez. That's Paulo Foster and back in the corner there is Morland and his brother Malin."

"Petey—my man!" Morland calls out.

Petey starts grinning. "Hey, guys."

Just then, Natalie's phone rings and she checks it. "I gotta take this. Make yourself at home, Petey. Why don't you talk to the guys and get to know each other?"

She leaves and Petey noticeably relaxes, especially when Morland comes over and hugs him. "You made it, kid," Morland tells him. "You can start over here."

"Is she serious about this whole thing being a family?" Petey asks. "Like—seriously?"

"You better believe it," Baner rumbles. "You got any problems? You go talk to her and she'll hook you up. Her door is always open. We've all been there and she's come through for us all."

"Shit, I would be back in the pen now if not for her," Rocker adds. "The security guards found me sleeping on the floor down here when I first got out because I couldn't pay the rent. She gave me the money out of her own pocket to cover me until payday. Then she took me upstairs to that big fancy office of hers and gave me a lesson on how to budget my pay so it never happened again. She's an angel."

"I started washing dishes in the kitchen," Fernando chimes in. "I didn't want to go to the company barbecue because I thought I was the only ex-con on the staff. She found out that I didn't have the money to take the bus to the barbecue so she picked me up and drove me in her car. Then she transferred me down here so I would know I wasn't the only one."

Petey can't stop staring at each man as they tell their stories. "It ain't just her," Morland goes on. "They're all like that. You see a Triple Star employee out on the street and they'll do anything for you. It's every department of every hotel in the whole damn chain."

Just then Natalie comes back. "How's it going, fellas?"

"It's going great." Baner slams Petey so hard on the shoulder that the kid almost buckles to his knees. "You're gonna fit right in, son."

Petey keeps staring at everyone with huge eyes. He's in heaven. "There you go, Petey," she tells him. "You can start at eight o'clock on Monday morning. Oh, hey!" She checks something on her phone. "You live in Oak Park. You can ride the bus with Fernando here."

"You bet," Fernando replies. "Do you have a discount card, homey?"

"What's a discount card?" Petey asks.

"You get it from the bus driver and you get half off your bus fare. Which stop do you get on at?"

"He lives on Seventh Avenue," Natalie replies. "He'll be getting on at the corner of Patterson and Seventh."

Fernando nods. "I'll already be on the bus. I'll talk to the driver when you get on and you can get a card then. It saves money on bus fare."

"Thanks, man," Petey breathes.

"Sure," Fernando replies. "Anything."

Petey leaves and then Natalie goes through the whole operation of hugging all the guys, talking to them about their lives, and getting the details on any issues they're having, even ones that aren't work-related.

"I have a meeting this afternoon," she tells me once we get back in the elevator. "I'll be in my office for the rest of the afternoon preparing for that, so you sticking around probably won't help you at all. Do you want to see anything else while you're here?"

"I think I've seen enough. Thank you for your time."

"I didn't really do anything, but maybe now you understand a little better how we do things around here."

"Yes, I do." I find myself studying her. I still don't understand her as well as I'd like to, but I'm starting to get the picture.

We step out on the ground floor near the reception desk. She stops and turns her face up to smile at me. "Thank you for telling me your story. It's an honor that you would confide in me."

I shrug it off. "It's no big deal."

"It is. It's a very big deal and I'm grateful."

"Grateful! What for? I didn't do anything."

"You shared your story with me. That's big. How many people have you told?"

I furrow my brow trying to remember and then shrug again. "None, I guess."

"There you go." She squeezes my arm and smiles even more broadly. "We're having another company barbeque at Golden Hills Park on Saturday. Why don't you come? You can do another field study of our behavioral habits."

She laughs at her own joke and I find myself smiling at her. "Thanks. I'd like that."

She steps back into the elevator still grinning like anything. "I'll see you there. Have a good one."

She pushes the button and the doors start to close. "Thanks!" I yell after her and she waves before the doors close.

I turn away and head out to my car. I'm not sure what to think about everything I've seen here today, but she sure gives me a lot to think about.

Chapter 6: Wes

I get back to the office at four o'clock in the afternoon and sit down at my desk. I have a ton of work to catch up on, but I can't stop thinking about Natalie. She runs her business so differently from anything I've ever seen or even heard of.

It obviously works, though. I never would have expected that, but her words keep coming back to me. *You're running a hospitality business. Surely even you must understand the need to treat people well.*

It sounds so stupidly simple when she says it like that. I've been so focused on the nuts and bolts of my business that I never really thought about the human aspect of it. I didn't think it was as important as everything else, but of course she's right.

I don't see how I would introduce something like that to Monarch Resorts Group. We've had a culture of luxury, aesthetics, and making everything absolutely perfect and flawless for guests who want that.

I never realized until now that Monarch even had a culture, but we do. We've been cultivating in the background without ever explicitly saying it out loud.

That ethic trickles down from that top and that's me, isn't it? How could a family culture trickle down from the top when I don't even know what that means?

I see her doing it. It works when she does it because she values it and embodies it. She does it with everyone and they follow her example. They couldn't do that with me. Someone else would have to be that person if we did it here.

My mind immediately switches to her. She could teach Monarch how to be as close as they are at Triple Star, but she's made it pretty clear that she's happy where she is. She's also made it clear that she isn't about to help Monarch become an even stronger competitor against the company she loves.

She must love it if she treats all her staff as the most important people in her life. The miracle is that she can do it with so many people.

She doesn't seem capable of doing anything else. She doesn't seem capable of treating anyone with anything less than total respect and high regard. She even treated that young ex-con that way and boy, did it work with him.

I go through as much of my work as I can, and by the time six o'clock rolls around, I still have so much piled up that I stay late. Everyone else leaves the building. Now I can concentrate on getting this done alone.

I have my head buried so deeply in what I'm doing that I don't hear someone approaching my office. I jolt out of my thoughts when someone knocks on the door.

"Come in!" I call.

My Chief Operations Officer, Jules Hill, lets himself in and closes the door behind him—as if someone might possibly hear what we're going to talk about.

He keeps looking back and forth for hidden enemies while he inches toward my desk. "Uh…. are you too busy to talk?"

"Not at all." I am, but if he's coming into my office at this time of night, I should probably hear what he has to say. "Take a seat."

He eventually works up the courage to come near my desk. I probably wouldn't have noticed anything unusual about his behavior if I didn't just spend the afternoon with Natalie.

No one would ever hesitate to go near her desk. None of her staff would ever ask if she's too busy to talk. They all know she's never too busy to talk to them about anything, even if it isn't important.

I see myself compared to her. My management style is so different from hers. Have I been doing things wrong all these years?

Jules takes a folded piece of paper out of his jacket pocket, puts it on my desk, and sits down in the chair opposite me. He perches right on the edge of the seat, smashes his hands between his knees, and stares down at the floor.

He's acting an awful lot like Petey considering Jules is a thirty-five-year-old man with a wife and three kids. He won't look at me and....is he shaking?

No one would ever shake meeting Natalie in her office. Petey kept his eyes down like this when he first met her, but it didn't last long once he realized what she was really all about.

I pick up the piece of paper and unfold it. "What's this?"

"It's my resignation," Jules mutters. "I'm resigning from Monarch."

My head shoots up and I stare at him, but he keeps his eyes even farther down so he doesn't see my reaction.

I scan the letter as quickly as possible. It doesn't mention any details.

"Do you mind telling me why?" I hear how cutting my tone sounds and I try to soften it, but I'm no good at this. "You've been with me for more than ten years and you've been killing it ever since you took over for Anderson. What happened?"

"I know," he mumbles. "It's just…. Sharon…. she had a pap smear….and then they scheduled her for an MRI….and they…." He twists his head far to the right and his voice cracks with misery. "They only gave her six months! I don't know what to do!"

He bursts into tears, covers his face, and totally breaks down right here in my office.

I gape at him in horror. I have no idea what to do about this. What do you say to someone going through this?

How would Natalie handle this? She would know exactly what to say and what to do.

Doing what she would do feels so alien and awkward that I'm not sure I can actually go through with it.

I need to start learning from her, though. Maybe she's right and what affects him affects me at a human level. I don't see how what's wrong with his wife can affect me except to rob me of one of my most valuable executives, but what do I know?

I stand up and walk around my desk. I still hesitate to do this, but how else am I supposed to learn?

I sit against the edge of the desk, lay my hand on his shoulder, and squeeze. He collapses even more and his whole body quakes with silent sobs. He keeps his head craned hard to the right, but nothing can stop me from seeing this.

"I'm sorry!" he chokes. "I hate letting you down like this, but…. I have to! I don't know what I'm gonna do! I just…."

"You aren't letting me down, man. You've given me everything for ten years. You could never let me down."

"I'm sorry!" he repeats. "I don't want to leave…but I have to."

"I know, but I can't accept this." I take the letter and tear it up. "I can't accept your resignation."

His head snaps around and he stares at me through eyes brimming with tears. "But.... I have to.... I have to take care of her....and the kids and everything...."

"I know, but you don't have to resign. You can take six months of paid emergency family leave. If she's still with us then, we can talk about giving you an extension. Mike Reed is a good deputy. He can cover for you. You go home and take care of your wife and kids. Don't worry about us. You come see me when you're ready to get back to work."

He stares at me like I'm speaking another language. "But.... are you sure?"

"I'm sure. Go home, Jules. Don't give Monarch another thought."

"But.... really?"

"Really. Get out of here, Jules. It's getting late."

He blinks once and then, lightning quick, he grabs my hand. "Thank you! Thank you so much! Oh, my God! Thank you so much!"

I squeeze his hand praying to Christ Almighty he doesn't start kissing it or something awful like that.

He bursts out laughing in relief and bolts out of my office still yelling, "Thank you! Oh, my God! Thank you!" over his shoulder before the door shuts.

I go sit down at my desk. Thank the stars that's over. I don't think I can handle doing things Natalie's way, but he sure appreciated it.

I have another whole new raft of work to do, now that he's leaving. I have to transfer all his responsibilities to his deputy and put through all the paperwork for his leave.

Doing it Natalie's way feels weird, but maybe it isn't as bad as it seems. No one has ever thanked me the way he just did.

Maybe there's a dimension to this I don't understand. Maybe it's a whole language I don't speak. Maybe that's why people are so stand-offish around me—because I don't speak their language.

Now I just need to find someone to teach me how to speak it.

Chapter 7: Natalie

"Hey, Nat!" Logan calls across the park. "Where's Godzilla this morning?"

Laughter breaks out among the other employees gathered around the barbeque. "Who's the lady that falls in love with King Kong?" Tommy calls from the beer coolers next to the picnic tables. "You better watch out, Nat! He'll be carrying you to the top of the Empire State Building soon."

More laughter greets this and I find myself blushing. "Cut it out!" I yell back. "He was really nice about it."

"He was only nice after you kicked his sad ass to the curb at that negotiation," Madelyn adds. "He can be gracious in defeat."

"It wasn't like that. He wants to learn from his mistakes."

"Let him learn somewhere else," Logan chimes in. "We don't need Robocop lurching around our hotel when we're trying to run a business."

Tommy sticks both arms out in front of him and goes into a jerky, robotic step as he marches toward the others. "We are Borg! You will be assimilated!"

"Anyway, I didn't win the negotiation yet," I tell them. "The Farmers still haven't decided who they want to sell the Summit Hotel to. I have to go back there next week to talk to them again."

"Is Davy Jones going to be there again?" Sergio asks.

I open my mouth to answer when Madelyn screams in fright. Her hand flies to her heart and then she points across the park. "Oh....my......God! He's here! He's here!"

Everyone turns around to stare and my heart flips at what I see. Wes stands by his car doing something on his phone, but he's obviously here for the barbecue. He's wearing jeans, a casual button-up shirt, and sneakers with no jacket or tie in sight.

I lunge for Madelyn and pull her arm down. "Don't point, Madelyn. It's rude."

"What is he doing here?" Logan growls under his breath. "He better not be here to make trouble for us."

"He isn't here to make trouble," I reply. "I invited him."

"You.... what?" Several people spin around to gape at me.

"How could you, Nat?" Madelyn asks. "He's the enemy."

"He's a human being and he wants to get to know us."

"So he can stab us in the back at our next negotiation?" Logan grumbles. "You shouldn't have done that, Natalie."

"Well, he's already here and I'm not going to throw him out. I'm going over there to get him and you all better be on your best behavior when I come back."

I shoot everyone a hard look over my shoulder as I walk away—or as hard as I can make it. I'm on such good terms with all of them that I can get away with looking hard when I need to.

They close into a tight bunch and murmur behind my back, but Wes is already looking up from his phone and he spots me. He puts it away and comes over to greet me.

He raises his hand like he wants to shake mine and then lets it fall without going through with it. "Thank you for inviting me."

"Just warning you that everyone is a little unnerved by you being here. It isn't the done thing to invite our enemies to one of these."

"I understand. This is great. How many people are here?"

He surveys the park with his sharp grey eyes. It isn't the kind of barbecue most people are used to simply because there are so many people here. These company events turn the park into something more like a small town.

"About five hundred," I tell him. "We do this about once a month just to keep in close contact with each other. A lot of people never see the employees in other departments or at other hotels besides the one where they work. This gives everyone a chance to mingle and get to know each other."

"It's amazing." He pauses to watch the laundry guys playing frisbee on the lawn. Other employees' kids run around with them and no one looks sideways at a bunch of ex-cons playing with their kids. "I don't think I could ever do anything like this."

"You're just out of practice." He looks down at me and I wind up blushing again. "Okay, so you haven't had any practice at all, but this is all a learned skill."

"Are you sure about that? I'm not completely irretrievable?"

"I guess that depends on whether you want to be retrieved."

I find myself falling into the depths of his eyes. He has a way of looking deeply into a person. It's hard to believe he's so cut off from the rest of humanity.

He's attractive in a hard, rugged, distant way. He reminds me of a rough, bearded mountain man who has been living alone in the wilderness for too long and doesn't know how to come back to society.

I realize a second too late that we're standing alone staring into each other's eyes. He doesn't break eye contact and I don't think I can look away, now that he's holding my gaze so steadily.

His voice floats out of some other dimension. "Would you retrieve me if you knew I wanted to be retrieved?"

"Of course," I reply. "Isn't that what I'm doing?"

"I don't know. Is that what you're doing?"

The blood rushes to my face. Is he dropping a suggestion or just making conversation?

"Hey, Nat!" Rocker calls. "Throw the frisbee back, will ya?"

I look over to see the frisbee lying on the grass near my feet. Petey is running toward me, but I'm closer.

I pick it up and wing it to him. He catches it and calls, "Thank you!" before he runs back to the other guys.

I wave to them and now I suppose I have to turn my attention back to Wes. This powerful energy between us makes it difficult. If I look at him, I'll probably get caught in the undertow of his eyes again. Maybe I shouldn't do that.

He watches the guys play frisbee and doesn't notice me looking at him. One of the mothers is out there chasing a toddler who has wandered onto the field. The little boy totters over to Baner and raises his arms trying to reach the frisbee.

Baner sends the frisbee sailing to Fernando, picks up the little boy, and sits the kid on his shoulders. Baner laughs and walks over to the woman who hugs Baner around his big body.

Baner leaves the lawn and carries the boy over to the barbecue where they start socializing with the others standing around the picnic table.

Wes takes in the whole scene without saying anything. Does he even want to be part of humanity? Is he so far out in his own world that he doesn't know what he's missing?

I motion for him to follow me and end up bumping his arm. I don't seem to be able to stop myself from touching everyone. It's just the way I'm wired. "Come on over and get something to drink. We have water."

He cracks a rare grin so I guess he isn't fully assimilated into the Borg Collective after all.

He follows me across the lawn, but we both saunter at a slow pace. I'm not in any hurry to get over there in case someone decides to drop an insulting remark. That's the last thing we need between Triple Star Hospitality and Monarch Resorts Group.

"Anyway, as I was saying," I tell him, "this is all learned behavior. People spend years of their childhood learning how to relate to people. It's understandable that you would feel like a fish out of water if you didn't have those experiences."

"I'm glad you think so," he murmurs without looking at me. "Sometimes it seems like I belong to another species or something."

"Does it? Has this been bothering you for a while?"

"Just since the negotiation. I don't think I ever would have realized there was a problem if I hadn't met you."

I whip around fast and stare at the side of his face, but he doesn't look at me. He keeps squinting out at the people milling around and playing games, but he doesn't seem to see them.

"I'm.... I'm sorry," I reply. "I didn't mean to throw your whole world out of whack."

"It was bound to happen sooner or later. I was bound to run into a business somewhere along the way that valued the human element more than Monarch does. It was inevitable considering that we don't value it at all. It just happened to be you. Then again, Triple Star wouldn't be what it is without you. It would have stayed the way it was when Bill Simons was COO."

I don't know what to say. He's opening himself up so much more than he did at our last meeting.

"I find it incredible that this has never been an issue before," I remark. "You're in the business of people dealing with people. Hotel guests and restaurant patrons want to interact with human beings, not robots."

I get a flashback to the conversation we just had. Robots. Wes is the CEO of Monarch Resorts Group. If he's a robot, he would expect all his employees to act like robots, too. No wonder Triple Star has better customer service and employee retention.

"I guess that's the difference," he replies. "I always thought that most of the jobs in a hotel or restaurant would be done better by robots. I always saw the human element as a disadvantage. I never thought of it as an advantage you could exploit to attract more customers."

That word sets my nerves on end. Exploit. He's still thinking about it as something or someone he can exploit.

I don't get a chance to say anything before we reach the picnic table. I get Wes a bottle of water out of the cooler.

The other employees shuffle their feet for a second and then Logan turns to Wes. "Do you know Jules Hill? I worked for him at the Turquoise Sands Hotel before I came to Triple Star. The Turquoise Sands is a Monarch property, isn't it? He was regional manager then."

"Yeah, I know Jules," Wes replies. "He's been my COO for ten years."

"He's a good guy," Logan remarks. "He was nice—and fair—one of the few that is. It's hard to find a good boss these days."

"Yeah, Jules is a brick, but he doesn't work for me anymore. He just quit."

Logan gasps. "Why?"

"He had a family emergency. It's a shame. He was great—very honest and hard-working."

"Maybe you want to hire Nat to be your COO now," Sergio chimes in. "She'd change your company into something you would never recognize."

Tommy smacks his shoulder. "Don't tell him that! We're keeping her for ourselves."

"Don't worry, guys," I tell them. "I'm not going anywhere."

They all laugh and conversation breaks out in different places. Wes drinks his water and stays out of most of it unless someone specifically speaks to him.

He listens to their banter. I want to study him, but I don't dare, now that we're surrounded by people. They already think King Kong is going to carry me to the top of the Empire State Building.

I can't look at him if they think something's going on between us—which there isn't. How would it work if I got involved with a guy who is so much bigger than I am?

I'm not getting involved with him or any other guy. It's out of the question.

He waves his water bottle at me. "Do you mind if I walk around and soak up the vibes for a while?"

"Go ahead. I'll go with you."

He wanders off and we end up strolling to the other end of the park. It's kind of hard to start a conversation when everyone keeps coming up to me and talking to me.

Everyone either ignores him or deliberately avoids him. I catch a few people giving me strange looks that I'm walking around with him. Maybe inviting him wasn't such a great idea.

"What is it like—living like this?" he finally asks.

I laugh and end up blushing again. I really need to stop doing that. "I don't know how to answer that. What would you say if I asked what it's like to live the way you do?"

"It's great. I don't have a problem with it."

"You must have a problem with it if you're here trying to learn how to change it."

"I guess I am."

"This is the only way I've ever lived," I tell him. "I can't imagine living without it. That's why we're all here doing this—because none of us wants to live like you do. It's the worst torture I can imagine—having no family or any human connections. I don't know how you can stand it."

He squints into the distance. "I'm beginning to understand that, now that I've met you—all of you. I don't feel it as a torture. It's more like a pain that has been there for so long that I don't feel it anymore—except that now it's waking up."

I stare at him in horror. Those words spark all the aching sorrow of my first reaction to his story. He doesn't feel it most of the time until some inkling of its true depth breaks the surface. Then he realizes just how deep and how painful it really is.

He glances over and a small smile creeps across his face when he sees my expression. "That bad, huh?"

I force myself to look away. Poor guy. He definitely needs to be retrieved. I just don't know how or if he even can be retrieved. Maybe he's too far gone. Maybe he's too damaged.... but that can't be right.

He wouldn't want to change it if he was totally irretrievable. He wouldn't be here admiring what we have like a starving man imprisoned behind a wire fence who has to watch a bunch of people feasting on something he can never have.

That thought makes my throat constrict. I want to help him. I just don't know how.

Chapter 8: Natalie

Wes and I come to the end of the park. The lawn drops away to a pond lined with trees. A bunch of kids from the barbecue are down there throwing stones into the water and skipping flat rocks across the surface.

A ten-year-old boy charges up the bank and throws his arms around me. "Natalie! It's so good to see you!"

"Hey, darling!" I rumple his hair. "You're out of your cast! Congratulations! Are you playing soccer again yet?"

"The doctors said I have to wait six months for my leg to heal, but I feel all right."

"Good for you. You'll be back at it in no time."

He runs back down to join the other kids.

"Hey, Natalie!" another boy yells. "Come on down! We're holding the Shot-Put World Championships!"

"You go ahead! I'm not good enough to qualify even for the quarterfinals."

Everyone laughs and I go back to walking down the path with Wes. I don't know how to restart the conversation, but a second later, he blurts out, "Are you seeing anyone here?"

I skid to a halt staring at him. "What?!"

"I wasn't sure. You're always touching people and hugging them and even kissing them. It's hard to tell if any of them is more important to you than anyone else."

I force myself to look away and start walking again. "No, I'm not seeing anyone—here or anywhere."

"Why not? You're so involved in all their families and everything. I thought you'd be married with a dozen kids of your own."

I laugh, but I can't look at him. "Naw. Not me."

"Why?" he asks. "What better way to have a family?"

I don't know how to answer him, but he doesn't push it. He doesn't say anything about it again. He just drops it.

That question hangs in the air between us. He'll probably never say anything again if I don't. He seems content to walk in silence.

"I guess...." I gulp trying to decide what to say. "I guess it's just easier to be everyone else's family than to have one of my own."

"What do you mean?" He glances over at me and now I feel those eyes boring into the side of my head. I can't look at him. I'd be lost if I had to face him right now.

I flounder trying to come up with something to say. "My dad.... I'm not sure.... it's complicated."

"You know all about me," he tells me. "I'm just trying to understand."

"I know...." I break off and shake my head in confusion. What do I say to him?

"What does your dad have to do with it? You said you were close to him."

"I am."

He doesn't answer. He lets that silence linger. I don't want to answer, but that silence demands that I give one. "Let's just say you aren't the only one who's irretrievable."

"What does that mean?"

I keep shaking my head as if that can somehow answer his question. I really need to tell him, but I can't.

The path flanks the trees along the edge of the pond. It curves to the left and then dips down a slope. It goes through the trees and then continues to trace the shore out of sight.

We keep getting farther and farther away from the barbecue. All those connections and the stability of those relationships dwindle with every step.

Out of nowhere, Wes takes my elbow and turns me to face him. His eyes leave me nowhere to hide. "If you know something, please tell me. Don't let me think I'm the only one that's stuck like this. What is it? Why do you think you're irretrievable?"

I open my mouth. I don't want to look at him, but now his eyes leave me no choice.

Looking into his eyes hurts. It brings up so many painful memories. "My dad...."

He waits. I can't say the words. I can't tell him. I don't know why. I wish like anything I *could* tell him.

He keeps staring at me. I try to look anywhere but at him, but he sees anyway. He doesn't need words.

Without warning, he takes a step toward me, slides one huge hand behind my back, and kisses me. I don't know why, but it seems inevitable that it would come to this. I'm not even surprised when he does it, and just like that, I start kissing him back.

He eases me closer to his giant frame, but he's so big that he winds up picking me up off the ground. Once he does that, it's easier if he just keeps lifting me higher until I hang from my arms around his neck.

His head and face and mouth feel so much bigger than mine, but he also feels incredibly good and big and strong and solid. Nothing can move him. I can kiss him without worrying about anything. No one can see us.

I wouldn't be able to do any of this around anyone from Triple Star, but I can do it here. His body flexes with muscle, his lips consume me in fire, and my body erupts in raging desire. I can let him feel and see that, now that no one else is around.

His arms dwarf me and make me feel small and vulnerable compared to him. His tongue slithers into my mouth and I feel him starting to get hard. He shoves me down on his huge bulge and I whine into his mouth as my desire skyrockets out of control.

I whimper in ragged ecstasy as he moves me back and forth on his knob. He grinds me to sobbing, panting delight. I can't believe I'm doing this with him, but it sure looks like I'm responding.

He slides one hand up my spine to my neck and his fingers thread into my hair. He crushes my mouth tight to his and his hand covers almost my whole back. He could snap me in half if he wanted to, but he's amazingly gentle and he never loses control.

His fingers crawl down to my ass, and before I think to stop it, he inches just a little lower and wraps around my crotch from behind.

His fingers clamp between my legs at the same time that he grips my ass in one monstrous palm. His sheer size electrifies me in unbelievable ways. I want him just so I can feel what it's like to experience a man as big as he is.

He massages my ass and slit from behind until I sob and moan into his mouth. Then, when I think the intensity will drive me insane, he jams his hand down the back of my jeans so his fingers touch my ragged, saturated slit.

I feel myself losing my mind, but the forbidden nature of this moment turns me on so much that I can't stop it. I don't want to stop it. I want him right now. I want him to pulverize me with his size, and at the same time, I know I'll be safe and protected with him.

He doesn't tear my clothes off even though he could so easily. He never loses control as his fingers drill into my deepest core.

He keeps his eyes open the whole time, even when I'm too drunk with unstoppable lust to hold his gaze. He sees me spiraling into oblivion and he watches me every second. He never breaks that stare as he teases me to screaming madness.

He pushes me down on his bulge and grinds me through my jeans while he fingers me to a frenzy. He's so throbbing hard and he turns me on so much that I can't stop the explosion. I drive myself down on his fingers and buckle screaming in a fast, hot, punishing climax.

He holds me while I tremble and spasm in his arms. I can't kiss him anymore as I shriek into his mouth. He keeps watching me through it all, and when I finish, he pulls me off his mouth and steers my head down on his shoulder.

He covers my head with one hand and holds me there until the last whimpering sobs leave me. I hide in his neck feeling the aching need that even this doesn't satisfy. I want so much more, but I can't let myself feel that.

He kisses my neck and ear and cheek while I lie there shuddering on his fingers buried inside me. He doesn't speak, and after a long, silent moment, he pulls his hand out and lowers my feet to the ground.

He presses my head against his chest. I barely come up to his sternum, and when he hugs my ear to his body, I hear his heart pounding in there.

I want to pull away and run from this feeling, but his fingers laced in my hair feel too good. I put my arms around him and shut my eyes. I probably shouldn't have done that, but I did and now I can't stop shivering with all the energy he wakes up in me.

I want more at the same time I know I shouldn't. We're business rivals. Neither of us has secured the Summit Hotel yet. I still have to negotiate with the Farmer family and that means Wes will be there. I shouldn't fraternize with the enemy like this, but I can't think of him that way.

He lets go of my head, and when I stand up, he cups my chin and starts kissing me again. His lips and tongue grip me in an unbreakable power I don't understand. I can't stop kissing him.

His lips and tongue and hand and body speak to me in strange, magical, mysterious ways. I don't know what he's trying to tell me. Maybe he's teaching me something as important as I'm trying to teach him.

He draws away, and without agreeing on it first, we both break eye contact and start walking back toward the barbecue. In a few minutes, we'll walk around those trees and everyone will be able to see us again. I almost regret that. I want to find out what secrets he could show me even as I shudder in terror that I might find out what he could show me.

I can't let this moment go by without doing something.... something big, but I don't seem to be able to cross that barrier. We get closer to the corner. He doesn't say anything. This is all on me. If anything changes between us, it will have to come from me.

The last rim of trees is only a few feet away. I shoot out my hand and grab his arm. "Wes.... you aren't the only one."

He stares into my eyes and I find myself swimming in their depths before he dives in and kisses me even more deeply. "Thank you," he whispers and then pulls away.

We walk around the corner and people wave and yell and call out to me. The kids run over to me, grab me, and then run off to join their friends. A different group is playing touch football on the lawn now. The laundry guys are all over by the barbecue eating and shooting the breeze with the other employees.

I follow Wes to his car and stop a few feet away. "Thanks for coming over."

"Thank you for having me," he replies. "I guess I'll see you next week at the Summit Hotel."

"Yeah." I smile at him even though I can't think clearly enough to decide how I feel about him.... or any of this. "I guess I will."

He smiles back down at me. That's the first full, genuinely unguarded smile I've seen from him yet. "May the best man win."

I laugh in spite of myself. "Yeah. See you there."

He gets in his car, waves, and drives off. Now I'm alone except for my big extended family. They're all waiting for me, but it would be nice if he was still here. It would be nice if he was human enough to be a part of this instead of always being on the outside, but he isn't the only one.

Chapter 9: Wes

I walk into the negotiating room at the Summit Hotel to find Natalie and her team seated on their side of the triangle of tables. They murmur in each other's ears while the Farmer family talks to each other at the top table.

I file into place with the rest of the Monarch executive committee and I take out my tablet to run through my notes even though I already have them memorized. The first negotiation was just the introduction. Today is when the real fireworks will start.

Natalie shoots me furtive glances across the room, but I can't read her expression. I better bring it today after she trounced me last time. If I can't convince the Farmer family today, she'll probably bag this hotel and this will be the first defeat of my career. I can't let that happen.

I underestimated her last time. I won't let it happen a second time.

My execs chat casually while we wait for the negotiation to start, but I don't want to talk. I want to get started. I can't sit still and the tension coming from both tables is palpable.

Ollie Farmer finally scoots in his chair. "Morning, folks. Thank you again for coming in. We started with you last time, Ms. Fahey, so we'll start with Mr. Winslow today. The floor is yours, Mr. Winslow."

He leans back in his chair and I stand up, but we won't be using PowerPoint presentations today. "Thank you, Mr. Farmer. Ms.

Fahey—ladies and gentlemen. As I mentioned last week, Monarch Resorts Group enjoys an industry-wide reputation for luxury, beauty, and status that Triple Star Hospitality can't rival. The family atmosphere and close-knit community that Triple Star is so proud of puts their business in a class that can't even hope to compete with Monarch's position at the top of the hospitality industry. Even if Triple Star offers similar amenities and aesthetics, it's this same family atmosphere and comfortable environment that will disadvantage its business model in the eyes of the very customers Monarch seeks to attract. Our target customers seek to distance themselves from those that serve them. Our target customers want to feel elevated and distinguished compared to those who offer them this service. Triple Star undermines this offering, and if the Summit Hotel assigns itself to Triple Star's community ethic, your business will be relegating itself to a lower tier of the social ladder that will prevent it from rising any higher. The Summit Hotel will always be a value-centric family enterprise with no opportunity to become anything better."

Natalie rises to her feet across the room. If I ever thought we could get through this negotiation without the knives coming out, that idea goes straight out the window when she fixes her fierce eyes on me.

"What you call better is nothing more than a venue for your customers to step on those who serve them. Triple Star prides itself on bringing customers and service people closer together. Your business model encourages your customers to view their service people as serfs and wage slaves in a different category of humanity than the customers themselves—or maybe your customers want to view their service people as something less than human altogether. Is that really what you're suggesting? Our guests are human beings. They want to relate to their servers as equal human beings who care about their wellbeing and who will go the distance to accommodate their needs out of a common bond of human connection. Your business model exacerbates the social divide to the point where you could never get the best out of either your employees or your customers. Who in their right mind would want to work in an environment where the guests completely ignore their humanity?"

"Our employees love working for us because they get to be part of something bigger, something grander—something that puts them in touch with the elite of society," I tell her. "Our business allows our employees to participate in an exclusive social status they could only dream of but could never attain without this opportunity. Our guests want to feel elite and we give them that. They want to feel that they're apart from the messy, degenerate aspects of society and we offer them a place to escape all that."

Her eyes pop. "Messy—degenerate—how? What aspects of society are you calling degenerate that you think Triple Star is exposing its customers to? Do you honestly think our customers would keep coming back again and again—getting involved in our employees' lives and staying in touch with them for years—inviting them to holiday dinners at their homes and involving each other in their personal lives if they didn't value the connection and intimate attention that we provide?"

"I doubt your customers would be so interested in all those high-blown ideas if they knew the class of people they were associating with." I turn back to the Farmers. "I have investigated Triple Star in depth and discovered that a significant portion of its employee base is drawn from disreputable and even criminal sources."

Natalie's jaw drops and her eyes glaze over for a split second when she realizes what I just said. The next instant, her features go hard and dangerously cold. "There is no one working for Triple Star in any capacity that is any danger to society at large or our customer base in particular. I challenge you to produce any evidence that they are."

"I'm not talking about them being a danger to society." Jim Kaufman, my CFO, hands me a file folder and I hold it up in front of the Farmers before I drop it on the table with a loud smack. That sound echoes through the room and Natalie jumps. "I have a list here of more than a hundred employees on the Triple Star employee roster who have criminal records."

"That's a hundred employees across our entire chain!" she roars. "That's less than ten per hotel and each one of those employees is working in a capacity where they never come into contact with guests at all! How do you claim they're exerting a disreputable and criminal influence on our guests?"

"You're running a business, not a social service, Ms. Fahey," I counter. "I also have evidence that your own father was convicted of manslaughter and that you yourself testified against him in the trial that got him imprisoned for fifteen years. He killed his best friend and business partner in cold blood and you have no secondary qualifications to head a corporation as big as Triple Star Hospitality in the first place. How does that recommend you to supervise the Summit Hotel or any other hospitality enterprise? You let your personal feelings and inclinations sway your business decisions to the point that they lead you to disregard the best interest of your parent company, your customers, and the responsibilities of your own job."

She stares at me with her mouth open for way too long and dead silence falls over the room. I might have gone too far, but desperate times call for desperate measures. The Farmers need to know who they're dealing with and they weren't going to find out from her.

She shivers once and wobbles on her heels for a second before she straightens up. She shoots me one last disgusted glance and turns to the Farmer family. "I will say this only once. If this is the kind of person you want running your business, then Triple Star Hospitality isn't interested in buying the Summit Hotel. If you honestly want to turn your family business over to a man like this, then you aren't the people I thought you were and Triple Star made a mistake trying to buy this hotel. I hope you realize what you'll be doing to your loyal customers and employees by selling to a man like this."

She sits down, pulls her chair in, and doesn't look at the Farmers or me again. Her team members lean in and whisper in her ears. She nods, but she doesn't look at them and her ears, neck, and cheeks blaze with heat.

A second later, her deputy stands up and starts speaking in her place. I never caught his name, but he speaks well. He starts explaining how Natalie's business decisions have led to such a radical increase in profits and that this is the supervision and business acumen she'll be bringing to the Summit Hotel.

He also points out that the employee profile I just used as evidence against Triple Star is a function of her management style—the same management style that led to this increase in profits. He points out very accurately that Monarch can't show any evidence that this management style has been any detriment to Triple Star's performance—quite the opposite.

I try to talk around him, but he outmaneuvers me at every turn. No matter how much I try to steer the conversation back to Natalie's questionable and unprofessional methods, he keeps reiterating that it can't be wrong because the numbers don't lie.

I'm having a hard time circumventing this argument when Ollie raises his hands. "I think we've heard enough, gentlemen. Thank you both for coming in. Thank you, Ms. Fahey. You've given us a lot to think about. We'll reconvene next week and give you our decision. Now if you will all join us for lunch, I think we could all use a drink."

Chapter 10: Wes

I head out of the negotiating room following my team and the Triple Star team to the buffet next door. I get close to the threshold when Natalie breaks away walking fast toward the stairs. She doesn't wait long enough to say goodbye to anyone, not even Ollie Farmer. I guess I made her mad.

I take a chance and go after her, but by the time I reach the stairwell, she's already three flights down. I have to run to catch up with her.

"Natalie—wait!" I call after her.

She doesn't answer until I get close enough to grab her arm.

"It was just business," I tell her. "I only did it to swing the negotiation. You can't blame me for that. I had to do the right thing for my company. I had to win. You know you would have done the same thing in my place. Hey! Turn around and talk to me. It was just business, Nat!"

She whips around and throws her elbow at me to shake off my hand. I have to dodge to avoid getting jabbed in the face. "Don't you dare call me that! How dare you suggest that you only did it to swing the negotiation? Do you think I'm that stupid? You did it to fuck me over! Get the fuck away from me and don't come near me again, you piece of shit!"

She takes off running just as fast. "I didn't do it to fuck you over, Natalie!" I tell her. "You were never going to tell the Farmers the truth about your background so I had to do it for them. They don't know you're hiring all these ex-cons and they have a right to know the truth."

"You fucking liar!" she roars. "Don't make it out that you did this as a charity move for the Farmers when you did it to serve your own selfish aims. Do you think I'm ashamed that my dad is an ex-con? My dad is my fucking hero!"

I freeze staring down at her. "He is?"

"Of course he is and everyone at Triple Star knows all about him....and so does Ollie! Who the fuck do you think you are? You wanted to shove it in my face that you found out about me behind my back. You wanted to throw me off my game so I would botch the negotiation. You knew you couldn't beat me on the facts so you pulled this out to undermine me. You're a fucking scumbag, Wes. I never should have helped you. Everyone at Triple Star warned me that you would use my help against us and they were right."

She turns on her heel and sets off down the stairs just as fast. I stand stunned by everything she's saying. How does everyone at Triple Star and even Ollie Farmer already know her dirtiest, most shameful secret? How can she have the courage to let everyone know that without being ashamed of it? How can she idolize a murderer and an ex-convict?

I have to run my fastest to catch up with her. "I took a big risk telling you about my background. Are you seriously suggesting that you never would have used that to win the negotiation? I can't believe that."

She spins around so fast she almost knocks me over. "Will you wake the fuck up, you fucking idiot? I wouldn't have used it because I didn't have to! Why would I use that when I can win on the merits of my company and our unique business model? I didn't have to tell them anything about you because it wouldn't have helped me at all. It would have made me look like a jackass for smearing your character exactly the way you just tried to smear mine. Do you honestly think Ollie gives a shit that my dad is an ex-con? Do you honestly think Ollie is going to make his decision based on that? Jesus, Wes! Use your head."

She sets off again, but not so fast that I can't keep up with her by walking. It takes me a while to decide what to say next.

"Why didn't you tell them about me?" I ask. "I thought you would."

She turns around and levels me with her most brutal glare yet, but at least she isn't yelling anymore. She snarls at me through gritted teeth. "Did you hear a word I just said? Using that against me hurt you. It didn't help you sway the negotiation at all. It made you look like a heartless, greedy asshole who doesn't give a shit about anyone and will sacrifice anyone and anything to get what he wants.... which is exactly what you are."

I can't stop staring at her face. I can't even really hear or understand what she's saying. Her enraged countenance transfixes me so I can't look away. I just want to keep looking at her forever even if she's this mad at me.

Maybe that's why I did it. I just wanted to get a reaction out of her. I wanted her to throw herself at me even if she did it in anger. I wanted to know I could somehow touch her and affect her in a way no one else could.

She doesn't walk away. She stands there glaring at me and seething with rage. How many other people have ever seen her like this? She's so nice to everyone and she handles every situation so well. When was the last time she got this angry?

Maybe that's what I wanted. Maybe I wanted to see her in a way that no one else had.

"Anyway, I didn't have to tell them because you just did," she growls and starts to turn away.

"What do you mean—I told them?"

"They know all about you now. You showed them who and what you are a lot more clearly than I ever could. You just showed them right now when you tried to smear me. You showed them that you're a callous, selfish, money-hungry jackass who doesn't care who he has to hurt to win."

I frown. "I don't understand you. What do you mean I told them? I didn't tell them anything about me."

She rolls her eyes. "Oh, for Christ's sake, Wes! You're a successful guy. You can't be this thick. I did an internet search on you after the barbecue and I found all the records on your time in foster care. Everyone already knows everything about you. Ollie and his family already know your whole history. Everyone you've ever gone into negotiation with and everyone you will ever go into negotiation with already knows. How many of them are bringing something like this out to screw you over because they can't beat you any other way? What is wrong with you?"

She turns and walks off much more calmly. She might not be raging anymore, but I really must have crossed a line if she's walking away from me like this.

I catch up with her on the ground floor and she heads off across the parking lot. "I guess I have a lot to learn about dealing with people," I tell her. "That's all the more reason I need you to show me."

"I'm running a business, not a social service, Mr. Winslow," she snaps over her shoulder. "You had your chance and you blew it."

She reaches her car, pulls her keys out of her pocket, gets in, starts the motor, and skids out onto the road before driving off. She leaves me standing there wondering what happened.

If she's right about everyone already knowing about me, why haven't they been bringing it up? I find it impossible to believe that she wouldn't, but what about everyone else?

I never would have dared to go into negotiation with anyone if I thought they knew. I really must be an idiot if I didn't think of this or at least look into it. What if she's right about me?

Chapter 11: Natalie

I come out of the North Star Hotel with Mitch Rudolf and Harvey Joiner, the site manager. "The fitting-out process is looking good, Harvey," I tell him. "Keep up the good work and you'll be in line for an early completion bonus. Tell your guys they'll get bonuses, too, if we pass the county inspection ahead of schedule."

"You got it, Nat. We'll get it done."

"I know you will." I give him a hug. "Give my love to Tanya and the kids."

"I will. We hated to miss the last barbecue, but we had to go to her father's funeral."

"I know. Give her my condolences and tell her to come and see me if she needs anything."

He chuckles. "She knows. Trust me. She knows."

We both laugh and Mitch joins in before they both go back inside. I head back to my car and get a notification on the way from Sergio. The head chef at the Celestial is sick and the restaurant manager is panicking because the Triple Star CFO wants to audit the restaurant's books.

My mind is somewhere else when I look up from my phone and see Wes standing by my car. He's parked right next to it and he leans on his fender waiting for me to come over there.

I hesitate to go near him, but I have to if I want to get into my car. What the hell does he want? It's been twenty-four hours since our confrontation in the Summit Hotel stairwell. I'm not as mad as I was then, but I'll never be able to trust him again.

I make up my mind and stride over to him. "What can I do for you?"

He bows his head and smiles down at the ground. "You always ask that."

"Is there something you want? We said all we had to say yesterday."

"Have dinner with me," he replies.

I snort. "Nice try. Thanks for asking. I gotta go."

"Where are you going? Why are you working at seven o'clock at night?"

"Is that any of your business? Go...do whatever you're gonna do and leave me alone."

I start to get out my keys and he comes over to stand by my driver's door. "Go out to dinner with me, Natalie. You don't have anywhere to be and you don't have a family waiting for you at home. Are you really going to go home and eat alone in that big apartment of yours? If all these people are your family, why don't you have anyone to have dinner with? Do any of them know you live and eat and sleep alone every night? Do any of them ever even ask how things are for you? Do any of them take care of you the way you take care of them?"

I freeze with my keys in my hand. I can't look at him, but I can't make a move to get in my car and leave, either.

"I'm curious about you. I've never met anyone like you," he goes on. "I want to learn from you and I want to learn *about* you. How many of your employees and co-workers can say the same? How many of them know the first thing about you? I'm asking you to have dinner with me—just once. It's one night—maybe a few hours at the most. Just talk to me. That's all I'm asking. It isn't a lifetime commitment."

I shoot him a death glare. "It couldn't be because you aren't capable of that."

"Fair enough. Come on. What do you say?" He glances across the street. "There's a restaurant right over there and it isn't owned by either Monarch or Triple Star. No one knows us there. Come on."

I don't stop glaring at him, but he's right. I have nowhere else to be and the truth is that I'm curious about him, too. Something about him fascinates me.

He's the only person who has ever put two and two together that I live alone. He's the only person who has even noticed that I spend all my time taking care of other people. No one at Triple Star knows about me because they never ask.

They never invite me over for dinner, either—not unless they need help with something. I go to their weddings and their funerals and their kids' birthday parties. They invite me over for Christmas dinner and Fourth of July barbecues in their backyards.

I get letters from guests and employees across the country. I get notes and cards from people thanking me for helping them, but they never invite me over just to hang out. They don't invite me over because I'm lonely and need company. That's the one thing no one knows about me—no one but him.

I glance up into those eyes. He understands a lot considering he doesn't belong to the human race. "All right," I finally agree. "I'll have dinner with you."

"Great!" He breaks into a rare smile. It lights up his whole face. He looks completely different when he smiles. He doesn't look brooding or dangerous or robotic. He actually looks human.

I lock my laptop case in my car and we cross the street to the restaurant, but I can't look at him while we take our seats. Why am I even dignifying this shithead with my time?

I'm still not sure and I have no idea what to say to him when he says, "So what does your dad have to do with you not having a family of your own?"

"You don't get to do that," I snap. "You don't get to just move in and start demanding answers about my personal life."

"I'm not demanding. I'm just asking."

We have to stop when the waitress comes over and places two napkin-wrapped forks, two menus, and two glasses of water in front of us. He takes a drink of his water right away. I should have my head examined for even being in the same room with him.

"Have you ever had a boyfriend?" he asks.

"Yeah, I've had boyfriends."

"So what happened? Why didn't any of them turn into you having a family and kids of your own?"

I guess I have no reason not to answer his questions. It isn't like he can harm me with this. "Well.... I work a lot."

"Is that the real reason?" he asks.

"I guess they just didn't like it that everyone else in the world can make a claim on my time and attention whenever they want. Most guys want it to be all about them. A guy wants to be the most important person in my life. He doesn't want to stand aside while everyone comes up and talks to me and asks me for help."

He listens without interrupting. He keeps his eyes on me while I talk. There's no question that he's listening and taking in every word, which leaves it to me to keep talking.

"I mean, if we went out on a date and someone came up to me asking me for help or just to talk to me, these guys would want me to tell the person to go away or at least wait until the date was over before I took time and attention away from the date to deal with someone else. I tried to explain that I'm not going to do that. I'm not going to tell someone who's in trouble and needs help to just go away and buzz off while I go have dinner with this guy and then maybe go home and go to bed while the person is maybe in a life-destroying situation. I'm not going to do that."

He furrows his brow while he listens. I can't tell if he disapproves of what I just said or if this is just his way of listening intently. How do I really know what he's thinking?

He doesn't answer for so long that the waitress comes back and takes our order. I get a burger and fries. This restaurant is really just a greasy-spoon diner. I don't see anything on the menu that a well-oiled machine like Wes could actually eat.

He surprises me by ordering a piece of apple pie with a scoop of ice cream on top. Now it's my turn to scowl at him.

"What's wrong?" he asks after the waitress leaves.

"Are you sure apple pie and ice cream won't mess up your mental acuity?" I try to make it sound extra insulting, but he either misses it or pretends not to notice my tone.

"I'm not at work and today is my calorie re-feed day so I can eat whatever I want. I like to treat myself on occasion. It makes the rest of the time not seem so much like a chore."

I don't know how to answer that, so I change the subject. "What about you? How come none of your relationships ever worked out?"

He shrugs. "They might say something different, but from my point of view, we never really had a relationship at all. We had some good times, but it never really came to anything."

"What would they say if I asked them?"

"Well, the last woman I went out with lasted seven months and she said that having good times with each other wasn't the point. She wanted it to become something, and since it wasn't becoming anything, it ended. My point was that, if it wasn't becoming anything, why try to make it become something it wasn't?"

"So did you want it to become something?"

"I don't know about that, but I would have thought, if it wasn't becoming something after seven months, it probably wasn't going to become something if it kept going. It would just keep being nothing—not that it was nothing before. It just wasn't what she wanted it to be, but if it wasn't that, changing it wasn't going to make it better than it was."

I look down at my hands. I have no idea what to tell this guy. Have his relationships failed to become something because he can't see what they would become? Are they not becoming something because he isn't making them become something? How should I know?

"What?" he asks. "What do you think of what I just said?"

"I don't think anything of it. It's your business if your relationships don't work out."

"Do you have any opinion on what I just said? You know a lot more about how people work than I do. That's what I'm here for—to learn from your expertise."

"Is that supposed to be a joke?" I counter.

"Of course not. That's what interests me about you—that you're so much more adept at human relations than I am. I obviously have a long way to go to learn how to deal with people."

"I'm not more adept at intimate romantic relationships than you are. You don't see me in a successful relationship. I've never been in a successful relationship in my life."

"You haven't?" He cocks his head to study me. "Why not?"

I shrug and look back down at the tabletop. I should take this opportunity to get as far away from this guy as I possibly can. I shouldn't be discussing anything personal with him. I shouldn't be discussing anything with him at all, but for some reason, I can't bring myself to leave.

He's right about one thing. No one has ever asked me these questions before. I deal with people all day every day and no one has ever asked me such detailed, personal, and probing questions. No one has ever been interested enough in me to ask.

His attention and interest are becoming addictive, even if I don't answer. I'm always the one asking everyone else how their lives are going. No one ever asks me. That isn't my function in life.

He makes me see a possibility I never considered before—the possibility that someone might actually care about me as much as I care about everyone else. He makes me see that someone might actually care about me *more* than I care about everyone else.

What would that be like—if I was the most important person in someone's life? What if someone actually cared about me that much—if they cared enough to give to me and never ask for themselves?

It couldn't be him because he's a selfish dirtbag who's only out for himself....so why is he the one asking? Why is he the one who keeps following me around and claiming to be curious enough to find out about me?

The waitress comes and gives us our food. I dither in confusion while we both start eating. Part of me hopes that eating will interfere with him asking any more questions. The other part of me hopes he'll keep asking.

What if he asks so many questions that he actually finds out what I'm really like? What if he just keeps on asking until he finally gets to the truth? What will I do then?

It's up to me if that happens. I don't have to answer any of his questions. I don't even have to be here. I can finish my burger, leave this diner, and never see him again if I don't want to. I can go back to work and go on as before.

Part of me aches for the safety of that world, but it's the other part that won't leave me any peace. The other part doesn't want to go back to that. The other part wants him to find out because that would mean he's interested enough and curious to actually ask. He would be the first person ever if he did do that.

He studies me continuously while we eat. He only looks away long enough to cut off pieces of his pie and he takes extra long licking the ice cream off his fork.

He doesn't ask any more questions—not because he isn't interested. He's definitely interested. I can see him simmering with curiosity over there, but he doesn't say anything. Is he planning his next assault?

I finally can't stand the anticipation any longer. "Aren't you going to say anything? You said you wanted to have dinner with me so we could talk."

He looks down at his plate and doesn't look back up. "I'm not sure what to ask you about. It seems like all the things I'd like to ask you about only make you uncomfortable so I don't want to ask that. I don't want to ask you about business in case you think I'm fishing for something I can use against you. I'm not sure what else there is and I don't really want to talk about myself."

"Why not?" I ask. "You're interesting enough, aren't you?"

"I'm not here for that. I'm not here to ask for your help. I mean, I am, but not like that. I don't want to be one of the hundreds of people that pours out their troubles to you in the hope that you'll do something about it."

"Do you have any troubles?" I ask.

"None that you don't already know about. Anyway, I don't want to talk about myself. You're much more interesting."

"You're only saying that because you know yourself much better than you know me. I don't know you so you're more interesting to me than I am. I'm not interested in myself."

"Is that why you're so involved with other people—because you're not interested in yourself?"

"No, I'm involved with other people because I want to help them. I want to make their lives better."

"Ah—right there!" He points his fork at me. "Do you think making their lives better makes *your* life better? You said their problems and struggles and challenges impact you at a human level. You said you want to help them and solve their problems because those problems are just as big a problem for you as they are for the other person. Is that how it is? Does solving their problems and lightening their burden improve your life and make you happier?"

Damn. This guy has a brain like a steel trap. He remembered every word I said and now he feeds them back to me. How is he doing this?

I can't meet his gaze. He's checkmated me without me even trying. Of course helping everyone else doesn't improve my life or make me happier.

If someone asked me yesterday or last week, I would have said that it did. I would have said that it brought all these people into my life and gave me a huge network of intimate relationships that nourish me and support me as much as I support them.

I can't delude myself about that when I'm with him. He makes me see how destitute and barren my life is. He makes me see how much I'm giving to other people without getting anything back.

None of those relationships lighten my burden. None of those people even know what my problems are. They don't think I have any problems except for maybe too few hours in the day to solve all *their* problems.

He doesn't push me to answer his questions because there is no answer. He already knows and he goes straight back to eating his pie like he knew all along that those questions were rhetorical and didn't really need an answer.

My burger is starting to make me sick and I push it away, but I still can't bring myself to leave. The spotlight he shines on my life horrifies me. I hate what he makes me see in my life, but I can't look away.

I need this somehow. I need someone to show me this. He's the only one who can.

Holy shit, what is happening to me? He's throwing my whole world into turmoil and I don't know how to get out of it. I'm not sure if I *can* get out of it. Maybe my life will come crashing to the ground and I won't be able to put it back together again.

Chapter 12: Natalie

The waitress comes back with the check and Wes snatches it before I get my hand halfway across the table. He pulls some cash out of his wallet and throws it on the table.

He chugs a bunch of his water and wipes his mouth. "Are you ready to go?" he asks.

"Yeah." We get up and leave. We cross the street back to the North Star parking lot.

He stops next to my car. "Thank you for meeting with me. I really appreciate it."

"I didn't do anything."

"I still appreciate it. I appreciate you taking the time to talk to me."

"We didn't exactly accomplish anything," I point out.

"I don't talk to you to accomplish anything," he replies.

"Why do you talk to me, then?"

"It's like I told you. I want to find out about you. I want to understand you."

I look away. "I doubt that."

He narrows his eyes and tilts his head to one side. "Why do you say that? Do you doubt my sincerity?"

"I doubt everything about you, but that especially."

"What—my sincerity?"

"No, your desire to understand me. You want to understand what you think I am. You don't want to understand *me*—not really."

"Why did you agree to talk to me if you think that? Why would you talk to me at all?"

I don't know what to say so I don't say anything. I don't know why I talk to him. I shouldn't. I don't want to think I'm only doing it because he's interested in understanding me.

I don't want to think he's the only person alive who *is* interested in understanding me. I don't want to think I'm so lonely and needy that I need one person in my life who cares enough to try to understand me.

I cast my mind back to work. I go through each and every person at the Celestial, in the executive suite, in all the other hotels owned by Triple Star, all my relatives, my friends, their families, my employees, their thousands of interconnected relationships....

What would happen if I sat Baner down and told him that I had a problem I didn't know how to solve? What would happen if I told Tommy or Charlotte or Madelyn or Mitch or Sergio that I was mind-crushingly lonely and I couldn't keep a boyfriend because I didn't know how to conduct a successful romantic relationship?

I already know what they would do. They would stare at me in horror—impotent horror. None of them would know how to help me. None of them would even be able to talk to me about my problem or to comfort me in the fact that neither they nor I knew how to solve that problem.

They would be terrified if I went to them with a problem they couldn't solve. I can just imagine what Rocker or Logan or Harvey would say if I tried to talk to them about any of this.

I can't look at Wes. I can't let him see how lost I am. He's the one coming to me for help when I'm the one who really needs it.

The problem is that there isn't one single person alive on this planet who can find me or help me find myself. No one can help me at all. I'm totally irretrievable. I'm completely fucked beyond repair and I can never come back from this.

I want to cry, but the true, vacuous horror of my situation is too scary even for that. In a few seconds, Wes will get in his car and drive away. He'll leave me alone with this gnawing void in my stomach that nothing can ever fill.

Out of nowhere, he places his hand on my shoulder and squeezes. He's still here and that somehow hurts the worst of all.

He twists me around to face him, and when I still won't look at him, he cups my chin and lifts my head so I have no choice but to look into his eyes. "I want to understand. I want to understand what you really are, not what I think you are. If you think I'm wrong in what I think you are, then I want to know the truth."

I wrench my chin out of his hand and force myself to turn away. "No, you don't."

He lets me turn away, but he doesn't take his hand off my shoulder. He's still here. He's still in contact with me. I wish he wasn't. Every second his hand remains there torments me with so much catastrophic pain that I can't stand it.

He lets the minutes pass, but I still don't leave. I could get in my car and drive away, but if I did that, I would have to break contact with the one person who actually wants to understand.

Without warning, he cups my chin again, swivels my head around, and starts kissing me. He doesn't hesitate before he dives in and kisses me with full, deep, open-mouthed kisses.

He does it so straightforwardly that I automatically kiss him back. His tongue tastes just as intoxicating as it did at the park. His lips feel soft and his body transfers his powerful energy to me so I start to respond.

I feel myself getting turned on and I rip off his mouth. "What are you doing?"

"I'm kissing you." He keeps his fingers curled around my chin and dives in to steal another peck. "You like it, don't you?"

I pull back a little more. "What are you doing? Stop it."

"I want you and I know you want me. Come back to my place."

"What?!" I exclaim.

"Come back to my place and spend the night with me. Are you on any form of birth control?"

I gape into the depths of his grey eyes. Is he really asking that? He treats it like a business transaction.

His hands and then his burly arms creep to my hips and then around my waist to my back. He eases me the rest of the way toward him and starts kissing me again.

He's right. I like kissing him and I want to spend the night with him. I want all of that and I want it bad.

He draws me the rest of the way in and my body touches him. He dwarfs me and makes me feel small and vulnerable and fragile compared to his mighty bulk, but the moment our bodies touch, I feel everything I felt at the park and so much more.

He excites me. He turns me on in ways no man has ever turned me on. I want to feel that rush of passionate pleasure he gave me at the park. It would be even stronger if we were alone in private with nothing to do but enjoy ourselves all night.

He kisses me deeper and his giant arms have the same effect of picking me up so my face comes level with his. It's the only way we can kiss comfortably.

He eases back without breaking contact with my lips. His eyes smolder with hidden fire. "Are you on birth control?"

"Yeah, I am," I mumble into his mouth.

"Get in my car and I'll drive."

He puts me down and we both turn toward his car. My body goes through these automatic movements without any direction from my brain. I want to do it with him, but I also want to find out where this is going if it's going anywhere at all.

Something has to come from meeting someone who cares more about finding out who I really am than he cares about getting something from me. Maybe he'll wake up tomorrow and this will all come to nothing. I don't know.

I want to find out. I have to find out.

He opens the passenger door and I sit down in the seat. I don't look at him when he gets behind the wheel and drives off into the night. I don't want to ask where he's taking me. I might seriously regret this in the morning. In fact, I'm certain that I will.

It's the forbidden nature of what I'm doing that excites me most of all. No one at Triple Star knows where I am. They would be horrified if they knew I was on my way home with Wes to do it with him ...wherever it is that he lives.

That's just one more secret about me that no one from work will ever know. It's one more pillar of proof that they don't know anything about me—nothing important, at least.

He drives for a long time without saying anything until he stops at a stop light. I freeze to my seat when his big hand comes to rest on my shoulder. Then, without any ceremony or introduction at all, he slides his hand down to my chest and starts squeezing my breasts through my shirt.

I gasp in a sudden rush of excitement and desire. His hands are so big and strong. He swallows my breasts in his hand and pinches my nipples through both my shirt and my bra. I start panting hard and then whining in agony.

The light changes and he slips his fingers inside my collar as the car moves forward. He burrows down toward my bra and flicks my shirt buttons open one at a time to give himself room.

I can't help but moan when he crams his fingers right inside my bra and plays with my nipples right against my bare skin. His hands pulse with heat that radiates into my chest. Holy fuck, he turns me on!

I collapse back in the seat sobbing with desire. I can't stop myself. I need him so fucking bad.

He pulls my bra cups down so my breasts hang out of my unbuttoned shirt. He can see me practically naked in the passenger seat. He stops at another stop light, and with no warning, he dives his hand down inside my pants.

He stabs his fingers into my panties, pushes my legs apart, and slides his thick, strong fingers deep inside me. I scream as a wave of ecstasy sweeps me out of my mind. He drives in all the way to his knuckles and I dissolve in a torrential avalanche of rapture.

I rock on his hand feeling the terrible catastrophic power of my desire for him. I want so much more than this. He electrifies me beyond anything I can imagine and the forbidden nature of driving around with him while he plays with me skyrockets me out of my mind.

He keeps fingering me until the next stop light. As soon as the car stops, he tears his hand out, dives across me, and pulls the lever to drop my seat back. I fall onto my back, and lightning quick, he shoves his hand down into my slit again.

I lie back moaning and whimpering and screaming as he works me into a frenzy. His palm crushes my box while his fingers drill all the way inside. He hits every sensitive spot and keeps me spinning in the stratosphere for all time.

I can only spasm on the seat with my legs spread for him to do what he wants with me. I want everything he can do to me. I want him to drive me around all night making me scream for him. If that's all he wants, then that's all I want, too.

He stops the car again and my glazed eyes open just enough to see that we're in an underground parking garage.

He switches off the motor and attacks me as never before. He gives me several rapid, biting kisses before he rips away and dives for my breasts. He sucks them so ravenously that I wind up shrieking and convulsing on the seat as his fingers still occupy my deepest secret recesses.

He breaks off from my breasts, too, and pulls his hand out of my pants only to take hold of my waistband. He pushes my pants down as far as the tops of my thighs and buries his face upside down between my legs.

My pants hold my thighs together and he doesn't try to spread them. He takes a huge mouthful of my swollen, twitching flesh and tortures me with his tongue. He kneels next to my chair, wraps his big arms around my hips, and pulls me into his mouth.

His tongue catapults me to the stars and I scream my loudest when his fingers creep under my ass and plunge all the way in again. He doesn't stop until my juices ooze onto his knuckles and I collapse back on the seat sobbing and crying. I can't take this. What did I sign up for by agreeing to this?

He straightens up and turns around to kiss me. His face smells pungent and fruity and the same smell comes from his hands. I sink into his kiss trying to find some shelter from this storm—the storm of how I feel about him.

He pulls away long before I'm finished kissing him. "Come upstairs," he tells me.

Chapter 13: Natalie

Wes gets out of the car and I shimmy back into my pants and button my shirt while he walks around the car to open my door for me. I get out and he takes my hand walking me toward an elevator in the corner.

He doesn't say anything and I make sure not to look at him on our way upstairs. I don't know what's going to happen there, but it sure looks like we're actually doing this. *I'm* doing this. I'm going home with him to spend the night with him.

The elevator doors open on the top floor and he leads me down a carpeted hall. It's dark except for wall sconces on the walls. The building looks nice, but not as nice as I would expect a filthy-rich CEO like him to live in.

I expected him to have a penthouse covering the whole top floor of a skyscraper. I expected him to have a private elevator or maybe even a car elevator.

Instead, he opens his apartment with a key just like a normal person. He switches on the light and a series of floor lamps reveal a medium-sized apartment much smaller than what I would expect for someone as important and successful as he is. This apartment doesn't even look as big as mine.

He throws his keys on a table by the door and lays his jacket on a chair. "Do you want something to drink?"

"You mean something besides water?"

He snorts with laughter. He actually looks happy to be here. He looks much more relaxed and at ease with everything.

He goes over to the open-plan kitchen that's part of the living room and opens the fridge. "I have tomato juice, regular cow's milk, coffee, tea, almond milk, and pineapple juice—no booze, though. Sorry."

"You said you only drink water."

"These are all ingredients for smoothies I drink for breakfast every morning—except for the coffee and tea. I keep them for guests. What would you like?"

"Pineapple juice, I guess. Thanks."

I wander around his apartment while he pours the juice into a glass and adds ice. I only see two bedrooms coming off the living room.

One has a large queen bed in it, but it isn't nearly as luxurious as I would expect for him. It almost looks monkish in its simplicity. His apartment doesn't have any of the trappings of wealth that most executives tend to accumulate once they hit the big time.

The other bedroom doesn't have a bed in it at all. Trestle tables stand in rows with a large desk in the far corner. Three computer monitors sit on the desk with an enormous stack of electronic components on the floor beneath it.

I stop on the threshold looking in. Piles of papers cover every table all over the room, but the piles are all neatly arranged. Paperclips, rubber bands, and a few plastic display sleeves organize the labeled file folders into orderly stacks.

Some of the papers look like official documents. Others are photographs, maps, or technical drawings. I find myself stepping inside and I cross to the nearest table.

The top sheet is a photograph of a car with its front half crushed against a tree. Police cordon tape surrounds the crash site and several triangular plastic markers with numbers on them indicate different spots around the car, on the ground, and even inside the passenger compartment.

My eyes flick to the next stack along. The top sheet is an adoption order signed by a judge in Nebraska. What the hell is all this?

Wes appears at my side and gets my attention by tapping the juice glass against my elbow. "Here you go."

"What are you doing in here? Why do you have this picture of a car crash and....?" My eye skims the rest of the room. He must have hundreds of documents piled up in here and I don't even want to know what he's doing with that computer.

"I'm involved in a crime-solving group online. We investigate cold cases and unsolved mysteries all over the world. It's a hobby. Well, actually, it's more of an obsession."

He flips back one of the folders in the stack in front of me. "This car turned up on a highway in Wyoming. It had two dead bodies in the trunk—a man and a woman—but they weren't involved with each other in any way. They weren't even from the same state and the Police couldn't find any connection between them. They were both long dead by the time the car crashed."

He turns to another picture showing the painted outlines of people curled up in the trunk. Both have their hands tied behind their backs.

"There was no evidence linking to the driver—no prints, no hair—nothing. The evidence suggests that the car drove itself to Wyoming and crashed into a tree with no one at the wheel. The owner of the car lived in South Carolina. His wife and children claimed he never left the house for more than eight hours at a time the whole month before the car was discovered. It's an unsolved case."

I look up at him to find him looking right back down at me. He doesn't act like this is anything out of the ordinary. "What?" he asks.

"You...solve mysteries? In your free time?"

He laughs and his cheeks color. Is he blushing about this? "Something like that. We've been working on this one for about six months and we've been concentrating mostly on trying to find some connection between the victims since we already know who they are. The Police had fingerprint records on the guy and the woman was reported missing by her husband two months before her body was found in the car."

I can't stop gawking at him in amazement. This......this is his hobby? This is what he does in his free time?

"What?" he asks again. "Everybody's gotta have an outlet and this is mine."

I survey the room and he takes that as a hint to keep talking about his favorite subject. I've never seen him this animated—ever.

"I started investigating my parents. I wanted to know who they were and how I got into foster care." He swivels around me and crosses the room to another pile a few stacks down from his computer. "I still work on it every now and then, but since it's a personal project, I don't make as much progress on it as I do on the others. These other cases have people working on them all over the world. We break up the case and each person works on one aspect of it. We make more headway that way."

He flips through the stack. It includes birth certificates, social services reports, and court orders. I make a special point not to read anything on any of the documents. I don't want to know what he's finding out about his parents.

"And this one...." He snaps his fingers on a few file folders right next to his computer desk and then turns his eyes up to my face. "This is the one I started after I left the barbecue. You did an internet search on me and I did one on you. That's how I found out about your dad going to prison for murdering his business partner. I didn't find out anything else because the whole case was sealed."

Those words land on my shoulders with an unbearable weight. His eyes burn down at me with so much power that I can't breathe. He's been investigating me. Is that why he's interested in me—because my background is a mystery for him to solve?

"If you don't want to go through with this, I'll take you back to your car," he tells me and casts a glance around the room. "Not many people have been in here—not anyone I wanted to spend the night with, anyway."

"Didn't your previous girlfriends ever come in here?"

"Naw! They weren't interested in any of this."

"You mean...." Now it's my turn to look around. "They never even asked.... or looked?"

"No. They usually just did their own thing while I vanished into here. I can get lost in here for hours. Maybe that's why they thought I wasn't interested in anything else."

"*Are* you interested in something else? Would you want it to become something more if it went that far?"

He shrugs. "I don't know. I guess I would have to see if it went there before I knew if I wanted it. I wouldn't know that since nothing has ever gone that far."

I find myself studying him. He interests me as much as I interest him. He's a mystery—a puzzle. What would solve that puzzle?

What's the solution to his problem? Does he even have one? How would he know if a potential relationship was made to develop into something serious if it didn't actually develop into something serious? How would I know?

How could any third party judge whether his relationships failed because there's something wrong with him or because they just didn't have the potential to become something more?

If his girlfriends went off and did their own thing while he got lost in here for hours, maybe they weren't interested enough in him to make it work. Maybe none of that is his fault.

He stands before me letting me stare at him. He doesn't try to kiss me or touch me or take it anywhere. Is he waiting for me to decide if I want him to drive me back to my car?

I get a rush of adrenaline when I think about him playing with me in his car while he drove across town. That is the hottest thing I've ever done and it was totally forbidden. No one will ever find out that I did it.

Will he play with me again if I tell him I want to leave now? Will he make me scream while he drives me back to my car?

A charge of hot, wet, smoking desire sears me between my legs when I think about that. I want him. I want him now and I want all of him. I want him all night. I just can't bring myself to cross the last few inches to where he stands.

Is he waiting for me to make the first move? Maybe he'll never make the first move ever again. I can't stand that. I didn't come here to back out on this. I came here because I wanted to spend the night with him.

I walk over to him, but he still doesn't move. He stands impassively while I put my juice on the nearest table. I make sure to place it far enough away from his papers so the dew on the glass won't damage any of them. I don't want to annoy him by being careless.

I extend my hand to him, but when he still doesn't budge, I end up laying my hand on his stomach. He's so big and broad and powerful. He stands before me like a mountain. Does he feel anything when I touch him?

I glide my hand up his chest. His chest rises and falls with his breathing, and when I drag my hand across his chest and back down to his stomach, his breathing changes. It gets shorter, more labored, and his nostrils flare. He wants me. He's getting as excited as I am.

Seeing him struggle to hold himself back arouses me even more. I want to make him respond to me the way I responded to him.

I take one more step and stop right in front of him where he glares down at me from above. His body pulsates with suppressed power and his shoulders rise and fall with every breath. He has to fight to control himself. Fuck, he's beyond hot!

I rake my fingertips across his stomach and graze his belt. His package throbs right under his zipper. I want to touch him. I want to tease him and make him moan. I want to taste him and make him explode because he wants me so bad.

I ease up close to him, but I can't kiss him if he doesn't bend down. He's too tall for me to reach him from here and he doesn't bend down. He towers over me seething with sexual energy. He thrills me and he's right here in front of me for me to touch him and excite him even more.

I slip my hands under his jacket and then under his t-shirt. His body shivers with hidden energy when I stroke his bare skin in the dark silence under his arms and up his back. His eyes drift shut for a second before he forces them open to look down at me.

His nostrils flare with every breath now and he breathes in quick, short bursts. I love making him want me. I want to make him feel how much I want him—as much as I wanted him in the car.

I want him to play with me like that. I want him to own me that way and make me crave him. He's doing a pretty good job of making me crave him just by standing here doing nothing.

I tug his shirt up, and since I can't kiss him on the mouth, I kiss his chest and stomach instead. His breath rasps louder and his hand flies to the back of my head. His fingers mess up my hair following my head back and forth across his skin.

I love the sounds he's making. I inch lower and take hold of his belt, but at that moment, he pulls me away and tips me up so he can kiss me.

He kisses me madly, hungrily, insanely. He stops just long enough to yank his shirt off. He looks massive and dangerous with his shirt off, but the next second, he goes at my mouth again like he has to steal every kiss while he can.

He picks me up by the armpits, turns into his bedroom, and sets my feet on the bed so I'm taller than he is. He has to crane his head back to kiss me and I look down at him from above. Is this how it is for him?

I catch sight of his eyes, and for no reason, we both laugh at this bizarre situation before he attacks my mouth again. He kisses me at desperate speed while he peels my clothes off.

He pulls off my jacket, unbuttons my shirt, and pushes it open before he falls on my breasts as rabidly as he did in the car. He sucks, nibbles, and bites until I scream all over again. I try to hold onto his head, but he doesn't make it easy tearing my clothes off.

He flicks my bra off and drops that and my shirt on the floor while he mauls my breasts with lunatic enthusiasm. I totter in an agony of anticipation, but he holds onto me so I don't fall.

He tilts back to kiss me and I get lost in his lips all over again while he kicks off his shoes and starts sliding my pants down. I know what's going to happen and I need it so bad that I can't stand it. I want to cry, I need it so bad.

I catch another glimpse of his eyes while we kiss and my heart twists. He's the first person I've ever met who doesn't make me feel like I'm alone. I don't feel lonely when I'm with him.

I'm not having Christmas dinner with him or watching the Fourth of July fireworks. I'm not talking to him about his problems or asking about his life, but being here with him makes me actually feel like I'm with someone.

He throws my pants somewhere and pulls his belt open without breaking contact with my lips. He doesn't break contact with my eyes, either. He looks straight into me while he rips his fly open and then he picks me up, turns me around, and sits me down on his lap so I'm straddling him.

I'm naked kneeling on his lap and his eyes tell me we're about to do it, but it's okay. He wants it and he knows I want it. It's what we both want and that makes it okay. It doesn't matter if anyone from Triple Star approves.

He kicks his pants the rest of the way off, but I can't see that. I can only see the bottomless intensity of his eyes and feel the velvet bliss of his lips and his arms wrapping around me.

His fingers trail through my hair and then his white-hot palm glides down my spine. Every touch of his hands tells me that it's all right. This is what we both want and it's perfect the way it is.

He doesn't take it any further than that. His rigid shaft lays between my saturated flesh and his iron stomach. Its pulses tell me that he wants this, but he doesn't take it to the next level. He leaves that for me to do.

I have to do this. I can't leave this apartment without doing this. His massive chest feels incredible when my breasts brush his skin. His arms feel huge and protective and warm. His lips swirl so deliciously in mine. I could just sit here and kiss him all night and he would be okay with that. I know that now.

I know he wants me. He doesn't have to tell me. I can see it in his eyes and feel it in every breath filling his lungs. He cradles the back of my head steering my mouth to meet his.

I don't make up my mind first before I rise on my knees and sink down on his rock-hard slab. He groans in rapture and his eyes roll back in his head when I sit down on him. "Oh, yes!" he croaks. "Oh, fuck, yes! Aarrgh!"

He clamps his eyes shut and his chin falls on his chest. He grits his teeth and stays bowed and grimacing like that when I start to rock on his huge size. He splits me in half and a tidal wave of pleasure and aching desire sets me off.

I pump my hips into him taking him all the way in. He keeps his head down, his eyes closed, and his lips pinched while he gasps through his nose. His energy escalates so fast that I have to speed up. I want him. I want to throw myself against him and feel that he's solid enough to take it.

His hands follow my movements for a minute before he opens his eyes to look up at me. His expression goes hard when he sees me riding him.

That look explodes in my brain and the sudden lightning bolt of realization rockets me into a frenzy. He's back and he's going to take me.

I drive down on him once before he grabs me. He circles his titanic arms around me and pulverizes me down on his shaft with strong, expert strokes. I scream as he stabs in hard and tight and then he takes over my rhythm. He doesn't leave me to go at my own pace.

He lifts me easily and drills me down on him while he covers my face, neck, chest, and breasts with scorching bites and kisses. He tears into my body with so much animal fury that I erupt in screaming passion as never before.

He growls louder when my steaming juices gush around his shaft, but he isn't finished with me. He crawls back on the bed, leans against the headboard, and clamps one arm behind my back to push me down on his masterful thrusts.

"Come on, baby!" he yells over my screams. "Come on! Give it to me!"

He tries to kiss me, but I'm screaming too loudly as one crashing wave after another destroys my whole being. I can't cope with all the pleasure taking me over and his strength overpowers all my resistance.

He keeps thrusting up into me from below at the same time that all this orgasmic energy makes me throw myself down on his thrusts. I can't stop it. I can't control myself as one spike after another shatters my brain.

He grabs my breast with his other hand and I feel his mouth kissing my lips, my face, my neck, my breasts, but I'm too out of my mind to do anything but straddle him screaming in rapture.

I hardly know what's happening to me when he picks me up, turns me over, and lays me out on my back. He keeps moving between my legs and bucking me into the stratosphere, but I can't stop staring at his face.

He rises above me, so huge, so powerful, so intoxicatingly magnificent. He's the embodiment of everything male and his presence sends me into a delirium of desire, passion, and deep, deep hungry devouring lust. I can't get enough of him.

I touch his face feeling the wonder of his cosmic perfection. His body flexes and ripples with muscular power while he fills me with so much drunken pleasure that I can't even think straight.

I can only lie here drifting in the heavens of all this magical delight. His body feels incredible filling me up and spiraling me out of my mind with one climax after another.

Every chiseled inch of him floods me with adrenaline and ecstasy. His lips, his eyes, his neck, his arms......

He raises one hand and closes it around my cheek and part of my jaw. He holds me there while he keeps rocking me in the endless bliss of this moment.

Chapter 14: Wes

I lie awake and stare at the clock on the bedside table. The numbers gleam in the darkness and give the only light in the room. It's two o'clock in the morning, but I can't sleep.

Natalie lies asleep in my arms. She curls in a tiny ball with her back and bare ass against my chest, stomach, and thighs. I wrap myself around her with one arm across her ribs and feel her breathing deeply in her sleep.

Her thin, delicate arm rests on top of mine. She feels so small and fragile. She makes me feel much bigger than I already am.

I have to fight myself not to get up and go do something, but I don't want to wake her up. This feels.... good. I like this. I don't want it to end.

I don't even want to go do anything. I never let myself lie awake in bed. If I wake up in the middle of the night, I always go do something. I work on my cases or I work on my business until I feel tired enough to go back to sleep.

I don't want to get up now and I don't want to sleep no matter how tired I am. I want to lie here and feel this. I want to feel her in my bed and in my arms. I want to feel what it feels like to hold her. I might not get another chance. In fact, I'm certain I won't get another chance.

She won't do this again. This is just a hookup to her and why shouldn't it be? I don't care if it is. Maybe it's just a hookup to me, too. I don't know why I'm even entertaining the possibility of it being anything else. I shouldn't....and I'm not. It doesn't work that way, especially not with her.

She sure does feel good like this, though. She's so fucking beautiful. She cuts loose when she lets herself. She's sweet and passionate and wild. I love that about her. She takes it hard and loves every second of it.

I could do it with her again a thousand times, but this is better and she needs to sleep. A guy can only send a woman to the stars so many times before she has to crash hard and collapse.

Her hair smells magical and delicious in my nostrils. I can't stop inhaling that scent and kissing her hair, but I make sure to do it softly so she doesn't wake up.

I love listening to her breathing and watching her features in the light coming from the clock. I love how she feels in my arms.

She stirs and lets out a shaky sigh. She scoots farther back and pushes her body into me. I hug her tighter and nuzzle into her hair at the base of her neck. She fills me with a feeling I can't identify.

All at once, she shudders and her fingers grip my wrist. Her whole body quivers and she shoves her ass backward into my hips. I jet of heat blasts to my crotch and I feel myself getting hard, but the next second, she wilts and falls back to sleep.

I hold my breath to see what's going to happen, but when she doesn't move, I bury my face in her hair again. She reacts instantly and wriggles backward in my arms. Her ass touches my shaft, and when she feels how hard I am, she corkscrews her ass into me.

I can't stand that and I grab her. I flatten one hand across her chest and the other on her stomach to steer her back into me. She trembles all over when she relaxes into my hands. Holy shit, she's really doing this!

She spirals her hips to encourage me and she whines in delirious rapture when I push between her thighs. She angles her legs to take me inside her and I succumb to the endless pleasure of letting her body swallow me in her hot, wet goodness.

She throws back her head and screams with every thrust. That sound gives me superhuman strength and I drill her to the core. She takes it all screaming and crying and spasming in my hands until I unload into her.

She buckles in my arms and her whimpering sobs fade to low moans. I listen as the last shaking convulsions leave her. Now we can relax back into sleep.... or she can.

She lies there sighing for a minute, but instead of going back to sleep, she twists over in my arms and faces me. She kisses me for a few minutes and then burrows down into my arms. She lays her head on my chest, wraps her arms around me, and gives one last long shuddering sigh before she lies still.

I roll onto my back and relax while she settles down. I love being this—this chest for her to fall asleep on. I love being the man she rides, the fingers she climaxes on, the arms she curls up in. That's all I want to be.

I run my fingers through her hair and massage her neck until her breathing lengthens. Her weight sinks into me and I stop touching her except for my arm around her shoulders. I want her to feel safe enough to fall asleep with me.

She only stays there for a few minutes before she turns her face downward and kisses my chest. I don't think anything of it until she kisses a little lower. She crawls her hot mouth farther down my stomach and I stiffen when I realize what she's about to do.

I lay my hand on the back of her neck. Should I stop her? Should I tell her to go to sleep? I can't move, and a second later, she crawls under the blankets and I gasp as her mouth closes on me.

I clench my teeth trying to hold back. Her mouth blisters me with so much heat that I feel myself about to explode in her mouth.

She doesn't seem to realize the effect she's having on me. She sucks harder, faster, deeper. God Almighty, I can't take much more of this.

She lies sideways next to me with one arm draped across my chest. She plays her fingers through the hair on my chest like she's fully relaxed doing this. She *is* fully relaxed. I can feel that in her body lying next to me.

She only hesitates long enough to sweep her loose hair out of the way and then she attacks me with that burning hot mouth of hers. I can't stop panting at the cruel intensity of her sucks.

I feel myself tightening my grip on the back of her neck, but that only seems to encourage her. "Baby…." I croak. "…. Baby…. please……"

She sighs softly, but she doesn't stop or slow down. Her lips crush me with their power and strength.

I want to cry, this feels so fucking good. "Baby…."

She doesn't respond except to dig her fingertips into my stomach. Everything she does blasts my head apart. I need her beyond anything I ever thought possible.

She swirls her volcanic tongue around me and sinks all the way down on me. Her throat constricts and that extra little bit of pressure sets me off.

I clamp her hard on the back of the neck. I try not to shove her down on me, but she does it anyway. She takes me all the way in and I can't help roaring as the dam breaks.

I crash back on the pillows groaning when her scorching lips slide off my shaft. She doesn't kiss me. She just lays her head on my chest, sighs in contentment a few times, and doesn't move again.

I stare up at the ceiling breathing hard. Did that just happen? Did she just suck me to the ends of the Earth and then go straight back to sleep? Is that even possible?

No woman has ever done this with me before. She treats it like it's so easy and normal and routine, but it was like nothing I've ever experienced in my life. She sighs and shivers like she enjoyed it—like she did it for her own selfish pleasure instead of mine. Is that possible? Can a woman like this actually exist in the world?

She snuggles under my arm, kisses my chest once, and her breathing starts to lengthen and deepen. She doesn't need anything else.

I couldn't fall asleep now if my life depended on it. I stare up at the ceiling wide awake. My heart hammers right under her ear and my whole body twitches with the last dying waves of pleasure that still don't subside even after she finishes.

What am I going to do with this woman? I don't even know what to think about her. Do I need to think anything about her or should I just forget all about this?

I lie here thinking a thousand things until four o'clock. I have to work today and I'm certain she does, too, which means we both need to get up soon.

I hate to disturb her, but I don't want either of us to have our days ruined by spending the night together. I don't want this to end that way.

I wriggle out from under her at four-fifteen, kiss her, and go to the bathroom. I come back out and stand in the bedroom staring at her for a while. She lies asleep and naked and gorgeous in my bed. What is this feeling? I don't want her to leave. I want her to stay here, but why would she want to do that with a scumbag like me?

I go out to the kitchen and make breakfast for her and a smoothie for me. I go through my morning routine until six o'clock when I take everything into the bedroom. She's still sound asleep.

I sit down on the edge of the bed and the mattress bounces. She groans and turns onto her back without opening her eyes. Her hair streams across her face.

She looks so different like this. She looks nothing like the competent executive she is. No one would guess from looking at her that she manages so many people so effectively and that she stands at the top of such a giant pyramid of interconnected lives.

She looks like a soft, sensual, luscious woman like so many others.... but unlike any other. I could sit here studying her all day, but we don't have time for that.

"It's time to wake up for work, baby," I tell her. "Sit up and eat your breakfast. Then you can take a shower and I'll drive you back to your car."

She opens her eyes and my stomach twists in knots when she looks up at me. I want her to keep looking at me like that—so vulnerable and delicious. Does she even remember the way she sucked me last night?

She raises her hand and lays it against my cheek while her eyes devour me with so much hidden, unspoken meaning. I don't know what it means, but I don't want her to stop looking at me like that.

She finally clears her throat, looks around, and drags herself out of bed. She sits up with the covers over her waist. Her disheveled hair falls to her breasts and her bare shoulders shine in the morning sun coming through the blinds next to me.

I put the breakfast tray on her lap and pick up my smoothie. I pry the top off and take a sip while she picks up her fork and starts eating her scrambled eggs. "You actually have real food here," she remarks. "I'm surprised."

I laugh and take another swig of my smoothie. "I have to eat sometime."

"Do you ever eat out or was that just something special you did with me?"

"Let's put it this way. I don't eat out alone. If I'm eating with someone else, I eat out. If I'm going to be eating alone, I eat here."

"Is that because you like to have more control over what you eat?"

I can't decide if I should be looking at her or not. "Something like that."

She eats in silence for a minute while I swallow my smoothie, but a minute later, she rests her hand on my cheek again. She runs her thumb back and forth across my cheek while she eats. She doesn't show any sign of taking her hand away.

That touch feels so easy and natural and spontaneous, just like the way she sucked me last night. She does it for herself, so she can stay connected with me. She doesn't need me to do anything but be there for her to feel.

Those small actions mean so much. I don't know how to feel about them, but they bring up so many strong feelings that I can't ignore them. What is she trying to tell me?

She isn't trying to tell me anything. That's what's so amazing about them. They're just basic, uncomplicated points of human contact, but they're so intimate and precious that they stab me in the heart.

I don't want to break that contact with her, but I finish my smoothie in a minute and now I have to take her tray away so she can take a shower.

I go back out to the kitchen to do the dishes while she gets dressed. She comes out a second later with her wet hair hanging down.

She looks lightyears different with her hair like this. She looks sultry and seductive. No wonder she doesn't wear it like that for work.

"I hope you don't mind, but I used your toothbrush," she tells me.

"I think I can live with that. I've already had my tongue all over your mouth."

"Are you sure my saliva doesn't count as liquid calories?"

I burst out laughing. "I think I can take a calculated risk on that one and say that it won't mess up my calorie count."

I have to kiss her, and the next minute, she starts putting her hair up the way she always wears it at work. The seductive look of a moment ago vanishes and she turns back into an executive who can manage the whole world.

I put on my jacket and hold her hand on the way downstairs to my car. "Why do you live in such a small apartment?" she asks when we get into the elevator. "You could afford something so much nicer."

"I just like it. I like to keep things simple and I don't want a bigger, fancier apartment that might distract me from my work."

"By your work, do you mean your business or your cases?"

"Both. This apartment works for me and the size and simplicity of it helps me concentrate on what's important. I don't really need anything else. I don't want anything else. I like it here."

She doesn't answer. I can't tell if she approves or disapproves, but that's the way it is. We get into my car and I drive her across town.

I resist the temptation to play with her body on the way. She doesn't need that before she has to go to work, but she sure makes it hard to hold back.

I'll never be able to drive anywhere with her without thinking about that—if I ever drive anywhere with her again—which I probably won't.

I park next to her car and turn to her. "Thank you for coming over."

She moves toward me instantly, cradles my cheek, and kisses me with mind-blowing depth and intensity. She kisses me fully and without any hesitation. She lets her hand trail down my neck and rests it on my chest while she kisses me.

She kisses me for a long time without pulling away. She kisses me like she wants me, but neither of us can let it go there. Did she love last night as much as I did? Does she feel anything—anything at all?

At last, she leans back and her eyes find mine. "Bye," she whispers.

"Bye. Have a good day."

She turns away. That's my cue to open her door for her, but she doesn't kiss me outside. The construction guys are still working at the North Star right across the street. Did they see her kissing me in my car?

She goes straight to her car, turns the ignition, and waves to me through the windshield before she drives off. I sit in my car for a minute and let memories of last night wash over me. I just need this one moment before I go back to work.

Chapter 15: Wes

M y pulse quickens when the elevator opens outside the Summit Hotel negotiating room and I see the Triple Star team already there. Natalie sits in her old place and her eyes shoot to me as soon as I get near the threshold.

She immediately looks away and carries on with the conversation she's having with her team. Does she feel half as nervous as I do about us seeing each other again?

I haven't seen her for a week since the night we spent in my apartment. I'm still not sure how I feel about her or that night or even if I should feel anything about either her or it. I don't know what to think anymore.

She hasn't called me or contacted me to do it again. I didn't expect her to, but I sure wish she would. I don't, really. I don't want her falling all over me expecting more. I respect her for not turning it into something it isn't.

That's just another point of confusion that keeps striking me at random moments. I don't know if I want to do it with her again. I would love to, but turning it into a regular thing might change it into.... something. Don't ask me what.

I distract myself by going over to the top table and shaking hands with Ollie. Every move makes me nervous and jittery. I feel Natalie watching my every move.

I sit down with the rest of my team. Now I'm facing her and I dare to glance across the table, but she's still steadfastly talking to her people. Does she think about me at all? Why do I even care? I shouldn't, but I do for some reason.

Ollie pulls his chair closer to his table and both negotiating teams face front to hear his decision. He glances back and forth between me and the Triple Star team.

"Thank you all for coming back in. It was a difficult decision, but we've decided to accept Triple Star Hospitality's offer to purchase the Summit Hotel. Triple Star's ethic of family and community resonates with us and we want the hotel to continue as a family business after we sell it. Congratulations, Ms. Fahey. We know you're going to do great things with this business."

Laughter and excited talk breaks out at the Triple Star table. The guy sitting next to Natalie grabs her, shakes her, and laughs in her ear talking fast.

I slump in my chair, but I'm not surprised. I went about this negotiation all wrong. Everything she said about what the Farmer family values turned out to be right. I should have listened to her, but I guess I just wasn't ready to hear it. That's the whole point. I didn't understand enough to know she was right.

She beams at Ollie and her cheeks glow with pleasure and triumph. "Thank you, Mr. Farmer. I promise that your family business will be in good hands with Triple Star."

He beams back at her. He's just as delighted that she's taking over his hotel. "I'm sure it will be. Let's have some lunch and you can get in touch with our office later today to finalize the details."

He stands up and comes over to shake my hand. "Thank you for your time. No hard feelings, okay? It was a tough decision, but we have to do what's best for our people—both our customers and our employees."

"I understand," I tell him, and probably for the first time in my career, I mean it. I only realized too late that he valued something I couldn't provide. Of course he wouldn't choose Monarch when he had Triple Star making an offer instead.

Everyone goes next door. If I had never met Natalie, I probably would have made an excuse and left after getting beaten by a total nobody like her. I would have thought sticking around and having lunch with the winners was just a cruel trick to rub my defeat in my face.

I don't do it this time and not because I'm anxious to talk to Natalie. I actually feel happy for her—for all of Triple Star. The best organization won. The right organization won.

It isn't so much about who won and who lost. It's more about who can run the hotel the way it should be run and that isn't Monarch. I don't resent the Farmers for turning us down. I'm actually relieved in a lot of ways.

I don't mind talking to the Farmers and even some of the Triple Star team. I find myself getting interested in them as people. They must be interesting if Natalie is interested in them enough to dedicate her life to them.

Then again, she's interested in everyone. Is it possible that everyone is interesting in that way?

That is so exactly the opposite of everything I've ever thought before, but if she believes it, it must be right. She's proved it a dozen times in a dozen different ways.

Hell, she even thinks I'm interesting and valuable enough to spend time with me. Maybe I'm not completely irretrievable after all.

I get caught up in several different conversations before I'm able to go over to her. She smiles at me when I hold out my hand to her. "Congratulations, Ms. Fahey," I tell her. "You earned that."

She blushes when she shakes my hand. "Thank you. Better luck next time."

I bite back laughter. I'm genuinely thrilled to see her again. "There won't be a next time. The next time I find out a hotel I want falls under your area of expertise, I'll be sure to stay far away."

"Do you have any prospects?"

"Not at the moment, but maybe we need to concentrate on streamlining our process before we acquire our next property. Maybe we need to reevaluate our methods and see if we can improve before we expand any further."

She bursts into a huge beaming grin. "Sounds like a good idea."

"How would you like to consult with us on the side—not as a competitor, but as an independent consultant?"

She blushes and dips her eyelashes. "I'll think about it."

I squeeze her arm for no particular reason. "You let me know if you decide to help us out. It just proves that your way is the right one. Congratulations. Have a good one."

I round up my team and head for the elevator, but when I get ready to enter it, Ollie calls me back.

He takes me into the negotiating room and shuts the door. "I just want to tell you that the bomb you dropped on Natalie had nothing to do with our decision. I already knew about her father spending time in prison and I already knew that she was in the habit of hiring ex-convicts for low-level jobs at her hotels. You revealing that in the middle of the negotiation didn't sway our decision at all."

"I understand that," I reply. "I didn't know until after the fact that you already knew."

"That's good. I wouldn't want any hard feelings between you two because of that."

"I'm not sure if there are any hard feelings, but if there are, they're between me and her. This matter is closed as far as I'm concerned and I don't have any resentment toward you or Triple Star for your decision. I congratulate you on choosing the right organization to take over your business."

"Thank you." He shakes my hand while he smiles broadly in my face. "I can see that your reputation may be overblown."

I let the matter go at that. My reputation wasn't overblown before this, but now that I'm aware of how I'm affecting other people, maybe I can start to change it.

I'm the only Monarch representative left on the floor by the time we get out of the room. The rest of them are all downstairs.

I head for the stairs to leave when Natalie comes rushing toward me. "Wes—wait!"

I turn around to see what she wants and she pulls up in front of me panting. "What's up?" I ask.

"Do you....do you want to go out sometime?"

The sun comes out and I can't help but smile at her. "I'd love to. Give me your number."

She gives it to me and I enter it into my phone, send her a text, and she sends me one back so we have each other's numbers. She smiles at me and her cheeks color. "Call me, okay?"

"Okay."

She goes back to the buffet and I leave, but I'm walking on clouds all the way downstairs. I'm going out with her!

Chapter 16:
Natalie

I can't help blushing when I get a text from Wes two days after the Summit decision. *How's the Summit Hotel going?*

I have to steady my hands so I don't drop the phone. *Still finalizing the sale, but it all looks good. They already have a family culture, so it's just a question of incorporating them into the rest of the Triple Star family. How are your cases coming?*

Pretty good. We found a connection between the two people who were found in the car trunk.... but you don't want to hear about that. Would you like to go out with me on Saturday night?

My heart flips. *Yeah, I'd like that. What would you like to do?*

Something where no one knows us so people don't come to you interrupting our date.

I beam down at the phone. He's so considerate. He always remembers and he plans to avoid problems I've had in the past. *Thank you. I really appreciate it.*

Would you like me to plan something? I don't know if you like surprises or if you want me to let you know ahead of time.

I wouldn't mind if you plan something. I hesitate and then tap out one quick question. *Will I be spending the night at your place again?*

I would love it if you did. You don't have to, obviously. Do you work on Sundays?

I can't stop my cheeks from burning. I can just imagine what he's suggesting. *I'm not supposed to, but I can get called in for emergencies.*

Good to know. How about I pick you up at your place at eight on Saturday night and we'll take it from there?

Great, I reply. *I'll see you then. Will this be a formal affair?*

Medium formal.

I burst out laughing. *Okay. I can handle that.*

Are you sure? We can make it all the way formal if you want to, but you might get barbecue sauce on your dress.

I explode in laughter and my EA, Marcy, who is in my office just then, turns around to stare at me. "Are you okay, Nat?"

"I'm fine. I just read something funny."

I get busy answering his text. *I can handle medium formal. Thank you for telling me.*

He writes back right away and makes me break down laughing again. *Bring your own toothbrush this time. I need to control my calorie intake.*

Yes, Sir. See you Saturday.

He sends back an emoji of a toothbrush and I send him back another one of an arm flexing its bicep.

He sends back, *LOL,* and I leave it at that. I'm going on a date with Wes Winslow!

I get through the rest of the week fighting down nerves. My life and my job are taking on a whole new meaning now that I'm living this shadow life that no one knows about. No one knows what I'm thinking about or what I'm doing on the side.

I always thought I didn't need anything outside of work. Now I'm finding out that having something secret, hidden, unknown, and excitingly taboo makes my life so much more enjoyable.

The fact that none of these people would approve of Wes makes this whole interaction so much more enticing. I feel like a kid who is getting away with something I shouldn't. He's so astute to plan something where there's no possibility that some Triple Star employee will bust me going out with him.

This whole thing just makes it so much more obvious that none of these people are really interested in my personal life. None of them notices me blushing and giggling and being stupidly infatuated with someone. None of them knows me well enough to notice me acting differently.

I don't have anyone in my life to talk to about any of this even if I wanted to talk to about it. How did I ever get myself into this situation? How did I ever let it go this far?

I don't want to change it now that I'm here—not with any of these people, at least. I don't want to change my relationships with them to reverse the dynamic. I don't want any of them to become the person I could talk to about it. That isn't my role in their lives.

Who would be that person for me? Wes is the only person I can think of. He hasn't asked me to help him since we hooked up. When did the dynamic between us change? When did I stop helping him solve his problem the way I solve everyone else's?

I guess it happened when we went to dinner. He said that night that he didn't want to talk about himself. He said he was interested in finding out about me and understanding me. That was the moment it changed and it's been like that ever since.

I cherish that with him. I cling to the idea that he wants to know the truth about me. He's the only one who does, but he never pushes me to tell him. He just leaves it alone completely.

I somehow white-knuckle it through the rest of the week. I pace around my apartment for most of Saturday deciding what I'm going to wear. Eight o'clock seems awfully far away.

I decide on a tight, knit-ribbed, V-neck dress down to my knees. It shows off my curves without being too slutty or revealing and I also leave my hair down. I don't know how he likes it, so I'll just have to chance it.

He shows up at the stroke of eight and grins like a fool when I open the door. "Hi," he tells me.

"Hi." I turn from side to side showing off my dress. "Is this too formal?"

"It's perfect." He slips his hand into mine and leans in to kiss me. My stomach turns a somersault when he laces his fingers into mine on our way to the elevator. He's acting awfully romantic.

Why didn't his previous relationships work out if this is the way he acts? I can't tell the difference between this and every other guy who wants it to get serious. Why did his previous girlfriends think he didn't want it to go anywhere?

We're way too early in the picture to start asking questions like that. "So where are we going?" I ask.

"You said you wanted me to surprise you."

"Damn it," I mutter. "I was afraid you were going to say that."

He laughs. He laughs a lot more now and he looks genuinely happy about going out with me. Is this different from his previous relationships?

He hardly ever broods when we're together. He doesn't smolder with radiating intimidation, either. Maybe things just got off on the wrong foot considering how we met.

We exit through the front door of my apartment building and he opens the passenger door for me to get into his car. I can't stop my heart from racing when he gets behind the wheel, puts the car in gear, and pulls out onto the road.

I sit tense and breathless in the seat. I'm so wound up that I barely notice where we're going. Is he going to start playing with me again? Is he even thinking about that?

He stops at a stoplight and I summon all my courage to glance over at him. He meets my eyes and then my heart stops when his gaze darts down to my body. Is he thinking about that?

I can't read his expression except that he clenches his jaw and turns back to the business of driving. I just wish I knew if he was going to do it or not so I could stop being so anxious about it.

He turns onto the parkway heading out of town. He doesn't come to any more traffic lights which means he doesn't look at me again, but nothing would stop him from playing with me if he really wanted to.

I can't settle down and I have trouble breathing for miles out of town. The streetlights vanish and he drives down a long, dark road for a long time. Only the dashboard lights illuminate his rugged features and he keeps clenching his teeth.

I find myself trembling with arousal as the trip goes on. I really want him to play with me. I can't tell if he even wants to. He grips the wheel extra hard and keeps his eyes steadfastly on the road. Did he even enjoy playing with me? I'm not so sure anymore.

He finally pulls off somewhere extremely dark. I can't see anything beyond the headlights except thick overhanging trees swallowing the road ahead.

He creeps the car forward and finally parks in the most remote, overgrown, pitch-black place I've ever seen. Did he bring me out here to slit my throat and throw my body in the bushes?

Dense, impenetrable darkness buries us the instant he turns off the headlights. He gets out and the dome light switches on when he lets me out on the passenger side, but it dies just as fast as soon as he shuts the door.

His warm palm slips into my hand. "You okay?" he whispers.

"Where are we?" I whisper back.

"We're almost there. Come on."

He leads me off into the darkness. My eyes adjust to the stars overhead as we make our way farther down the road. A second later, he turns off onto a narrow trail cutting through the trees. How can he see where he's going?

I hug his arm fighting down panic. I'm not dressed for trekking through the wilderness, but neither is he. He wears one of his pristine suits and he looks way more formal than I do.

He eventually turns another corner and we see a glimmer ahead. We keep going and the glimmer turns out to be a candle flickering on a single table set next to an enormous lake. A table stands all alone in the dark in the middle of nowhere. The faint rim of city lights shines far off in the distance across the lake.

A waiter in a tuxedo stands near the table with a white napkin draped over his arm. He grins at us and bows to Wes. "Good evening, Sir."

"Good evening, Charlie."

Wes pulls out my chair for me and then sits down opposite me. Charlie gets busy uncorking a bottle of wine and pours some into a wine glass for me. He sets another wine glass in front of Wes and I burst out laughing when Charlie pours water into it from a plastic bottle.

"Classy," I remark.

Wes grins back at me. "I gotta maintain my personal standards. What do you think? No one will see us out here. No one will come over and start asking you for help while we're on our date."

"Thank you. I really appreciate you doing this for me."

"You don't have to keep saying that. I'm doing this for me. I don't want anyone interrupting our date."

I can't help but beam at him. This really is romantic, especially when he picks my hand up off the table, squeezes it, and then holds it.

"What about him?" I nod at Charlie. "Who is he? I thought I knew all the service people in town."

"That's exactly why I hired him. He works for a Monarch hotel in another city. I'm paying him quadruple overtime plus airfare to come out here and serve us."

My jaw drops. "Really? You flew him in just for this date?"

"Of course. I wanted to make sure our server was someone you didn't know and that you would never see him again. He'll fly home tomorrow and take all his secrets with him."

I glance up at Charlie to find him smiling down at me. He looks extremely happy to be serving us tonight. His face glows in the candlelight. It glows almost as much as Wes's.

Gratitude splits my heart in half. I can't believe Wes is doing this for me. He's going to such lengths to make sure I can just relax and enjoy myself. No other guy I've ever gone out with has ever even thought of it.

Every other guy I've ever gone out with just assumed that people shouldn't come up to me at all. My former boyfriends got pissed off about it, but it never crossed any of their minds to do anything to prevent it from happening. They made it out like it was my fault that people relied on me for help and even conversation.

Charlie starts serving our meal. First, he gives us bread and butter plus salad. Wes eats his salad, but he doesn't touch the bread. "Let me guess," I remark. "You aren't on a re-feed day."

"Nope. Gotta stay on schedule."

"What happens if you slack off?" I ask.

"Not much except that I get disappointed in myself because I'm not being my best. It's more of a contract or agreement with myself to always strive for excellence in every area of my life. If I don't do that, I lose respect for myself because I know I'm letting myself down."

"I can respect that."

"How did you get into the hospitality business?" he asks. "You said you worked under Bill Simons, but you don't have any formal business training. How did you become Chief Operations Officer?"

"I just worked my way up. I started as a receptionist at the front desk at the Celestial. Things were pretty nightmarish then. Bill would constantly come downstairs and burn through the hotel like a banshee. He would bitch people out in front of the guests, throw food on the floor in the restaurant if someone got an order wrong, fire employees in front of guests and other employees, and just generally carry on a reign of terror through the whole hotel."

"Wow. I had no idea. He always acted so professionally around me."

"Oh, he knew how to behave around the right people. He never did any of it where any other executive or any of the directors could see him. He only did it with the employees beneath him and of course he was the last stop in case anyone complained. He made sure no one in the executive suite ever found out that the employees were dissatisfied and none of the executives ever figured out why the employee turnover rate was so high."

"Wow," he breathes. "That sounds awful."

"It was. I tried to help a few people and I made friends. Pretty soon, I started hearing from employees in other hotels that Bill was doing the same thing with them. He would go over to another hotel and leave the place in ruins. A few of the other hotels had mass employee walkouts after his raids."

He shakes his head. "How did you escape his vengeance?"

"I just kept my head down and never said anything to anyone that might be construed as a complaint. I did my job and stayed out of his way. While I was working the front desk, the quality control manager quit and Bill held one of his competitions to see who would replace her. He came to the front desk and told me I should apply for the position. I didn't want to compete for the job, but when the day came, no one else applied for it, either. No one wanted to compete, so Bill told me I could have the job if I applied for it, so I did. It was easy to get promoted back then because people were quitting right and left. The hotel couldn't keep staff for anything. After that, I got promoted to general manager of the Celestial and then Bill quit." I burst out laughing at the memory. "I can still remember how ecstatic we all were when we heard that Bill was leaving."

"Did you start this thing of helping everyone before that?"

"Yeah, by the time Bill quit and I got promoted to COO, I already had a pretty big network of friends. It was most of the people at the Celestial—at least the ones who managed to stick around for any length of time. We had a very informal mutual protection and assistance pact. We helped each other out as much as we could without getting on Bill's bad side."

"So how did you come up with the idea of this whole family culture thing?"

"I had to go visit the other hotels and inspect their operations, of course. They were all petrified of me. They were absolutely floored when I explained that I wanted us to be like a family to each other and that I was here to help them make the hotel as good as it could be. They didn't believe me at first, but once it started at the Celestial, it kind of snowballed out of control."

"That's amazing. It's hard to believe you turned it around so completely." His eyes sparkle at me across the table. "It's pretty impressive that one person accomplished all that."

"I had a lot of help. I couldn't have done it without the other employees. It wasn't too hard to convert the Celestial because we already had something like that going behind the scenes. It took a while to get the word out to the other hotels, but then some of the long-time employees at the Celestial made contact with employees at other hotels and told them that it was for real. Then it spread like wildfire."

He looks down at my hand and runs his thumb over my knuckles.

"What's wrong?" I ask. "Why are you so quiet?"

"I'm just thinking about what you said. It's hard to know what to think about it."

"What do you mean?"

"It's hard not to see it once you start. I didn't see it before. Now I see it everywhere. I can't unsee it. I...." He looks away across the lake. "I don't know what to do about it."

I open my mouth and hesitate. "What is there to do about it?"

"I'm not sure." He shakes it off. "Anyway, it's something to think about."

Charlie comes back and takes away the bread and salad. He clears the whole table and then starts serving dinner to me and Wes.

Charlie serves me a plate covered with an elaborate silver dome. He whisks the cover off and a cloud of fragrant steam drifts into my nose.

The steam vanishes to reveal a perfectly seared steak, a large baked potato heaped with sour cream, chives, and shredded cheese, and a pile of steamed vegetables.

"Thank you, Charlie," I tell him.

He smiles at me. "You're welcome, Ma'am. Would you like another glass of wine?"

"Um.... yes, thank you."

I can't help but blush when he refills my glass. He serves Wes exactly the same meal before Charlie retreats out of sight into the darkness.

I don't know what to think or say. No one has ever taken me on a date like this. It's so luxurious and exclusive. It's so removed from the whole rest of my life.

No one has ever created an experience like this for me. I realize with another jolt that this is the first time ever in my whole life that I've had someone's total undivided attention like this.

None of the other guys I've ever dated went to such lengths to give me their undivided attention. Wes only asks about me. He doesn't turn the conversation back to himself unless I do it first.

"This was really nice," I tell him when we finish eating. "Thank you."

"Would you like to do it again sometime? I mean, not this exact same thing, but something similar?"

"Sure. I'd love to." I frown to myself. "Have you ever done anything like this before?"

"No, nothing like this. None of the women I've dated have ever had your problem. They never had an issue with going out in public."

I laugh. "Maybe I should wear a paper bag over my head."

"Then I wouldn't be able to look at you like this." His eyes burn and his thumb keeps leaving a trail of sparks across my knuckles. "It just requires me to be a little more creative in deciding where to take you."

Questions crowd my mind, but before I can say anything, a high-pitched whistle goes off across the lake. A streak of light shoots out of the darkness and explodes in a shower of fireworks reflected on the lake.

Continuous booms and cracks echo across the lake as one starburst after another detonates in the night sky. They light up the landscape and thrill my heart.

In the middle of that, Wes squeezes my hand, and when I look over at him, my heart stops when I see the way he's looking at me. His eyes simmer with a different kind of intensity and he pulls me across the table to kiss me.

Chapter 17: Wes

I take Natalie's hand and pull her in to kiss her by the lake. Charlie has very intelligently vanished into the darkness where we can't see him while we stand with our arms around each other by the water's edge.

She keeps gazing across the lake and then smiling up at me. Her eyes tell me she loves this. She doesn't have to say anything.

Her lips feel incredible, and when I pull her close, her feet leave the ground so I pick her all the way up.

She sways when I move her from side to side. Her head falls on my shoulder while we kiss. She feels so soft and supple and pliant. I want to take her home and curl up in bed with her. I can just imagine the delights waiting for us there.

"Let's go home," I whisper. "We're finished here."

"All right," she breathes. "You'll have to show me where to go. I couldn't find the car again."

"Follow me."

I put her down and take her hand. She huddles close to my arm as we move away from the candle on the table. Darkness enfolds us and silence blocks out all sound except for her breath in my ear.

Her body quivers so deliciously that I end up pulling her to a halt under the trees. I have to kiss her and my hands find their way down her back to her voluptuous round ass.

She gasps into my mouth and then moans when she feels how hard I am. I want her right now. I have to tear myself away to keep moving toward the car. I don't want to do it with her here in the woods.

"How did you know about this place?" she whispers when we start walking again.

"I was in a foster home near here. I used to come out here all the time when I wanted to be by myself. I loved it here. I still do."

She doesn't speak again, and a minute later, I open the passenger door to let her into the car. I start the engine and put the car into gear, but just before I take my foot off the brake, she darts out her wicked little hand and slides it over my thigh.

That sensation sends a lightning bolt straight to my crotch and I jerk around to stare at her. The dashboard lights glow on her cheeks and reflect in her haunted, delirious eyes. She looks magnetic and irresistible, and before I can even move, she slips her hand farther between my legs and right up tight against my throbbing crotch.

I tense all over as she strokes me and then she leans in and kisses me for the ages. Her mouth and tongue blast me out of my mind as she squeezes me tighter. She prods me and pinches me through my pants to drive me to raging hardness.

I want to attack her, but just when I think I can't hold back a second longer, she leans back in her chair. She takes my hand, pulls the lever on her seat, tips all the way back, and places my hand on her chest right between her breasts.

She reclines back in the seat gazing up at me with such drunken, simmering eyes that I don't think I can keep away from her. Her breasts heave with her labored breathing and she contorts and squirms on her seat. Her lips part and shiver when she inhales a long, shuddering breath.

I can't stop staring at her intoxicated face. She moans out loud when I massage her breasts and then push my fingers down her dress to pinch her nipples. She whines and squeals. She really wants me to play with her while I drive.

I lean over her seat and kiss her. She sobs and cries into my ear when I pull her breast out and suck it hard. Her fingers lace to my hair and she writhes on the seat winding up to a screaming pitch.

I have to get her home and my package hurts, I'm straining for her so hard. I turn away, steer out onto the road, and start the long, torturous journey back to my place.

I don't have to look at her. I can hear her nearing the breaking point when I play with her breasts. I strip down the V-neck of her dress and push aside her bra so her breasts hang out in the darkness where I can enjoy myself all I like.

She screams when I pinch them and she claws at my arm in rabid madness. I have to touch her. I tug up her dress and she helps me hike it up to her hips.

I start by rubbing her through her saturated panties and then cram my hand down inside them. My fingers vanish into a river of dripping honey and she convulses on my hand riding my fingers.

She hitches her feet up on the seat and spreads her legs arching her back and screaming. Her internal muscles ripple down my fingers and I feel her quivering and twitching as she spikes off the charts.

She grabs my wrist and shoves herself down on my hand arching and spasming in ecstasy. She keeps doing that all the way home. I can't look at her or I'll explode right now. Her screams drive me out of my mind and her dripping channel feels sublime clenching around my fingers.

I almost regret the moment when I pull into my parking garage and switch off the car. I turn to look over at her face transformed with rapture. She stares up at me through eyes glazed with madness. I can't be certain if she can even see me.

Her lips form wordless, meaningless shapes trying to tell me how much she wants this. I quickly switch hands so I can see her looking at me like that while I pound my knuckles into her. I could stay here like this all night. How long can she really go before she stops me?

She squeals even more loudly when I work her into a lather and she grabs my arm as hard as she can.

She talks gibberish for a minute trying to tell me something. "You love that, don't you, baby?" I breathe. "You love giving yourself to me, don't you?"

Her lips shiver one more time. ".... Wes....... I need....... you......"

"You got me, baby. I'm right here with you. You like that? Huh? You want that? Huh? You want me?"

".... Wes......"

"I'm here, baby. I got you."

She loses her train of thought again. She's so far gone that she can't say anything else. I can't let it happen like this. I want her in my bed.

I draw my hand out very slowly and she lies there shaking and moaning for a long time while we kiss. Even after I stop kissing her, she still clamps her eyes shut and gulps hard before she pulls herself together.

I stroke her hair and pet her cheeks. I want so much of her. I want to take her upstairs and tear her apart, but I also want to protect her.

I never dreamed a woman could respond to me the way she does. She gets so turned on and she just keeps climaxing no matter how long I do it to her.

She needs protection from this cataclysm of her own desires. That's my job—to stop her from going too far. I don't know what too far might be, but I need to stay on top of that.

I make sure she's okay before I get out of the car. When I get around to her side and open her door, she's sitting up straightening her dress....and then she just kind of shuts down.

She looks down at her hands and just.... stops. She doesn't move. She just sits there staring into space.

She needs my help, so I lean into the car and kiss her. She wakes up instantly and kisses me back, but I only stay with her for a second. "Come on, baby. Get out of the car and come upstairs with me. We can't stay down here."

I take her hand and she follows me to the elevator. She stands at my side in a daze without saying anything or looking at me.

"Are you okay?" I ask as soon as the elevator starts moving.

She nods at nothing until I move in front of her eyes. Then she snaps back to reality and her eyes meet mine with that deep, yearning look. She almost looks scared of how far she actually went.

"Did I hurt you?" I ask.

"No," she replies.

"Are you okay?" I ask again. I'm still not sure.

"I'm okay," she tells me, but she's still in another dimension. I'm not sure anymore if taking her again will be dangerous for her. She really went out into space there for a minute—or several minutes.

She follows me into the apartment and I take her to my bedroom. I pull her dress off, sit her down on the edge of the bed in her bra and panties, and lift her face to look at me.

Her eyes communicate a mixture of deep desire and something like pain. I can't even kiss her. This flood of emotion going through me holds me spellbound. I just have to keep gazing into those eyes.

No woman has ever wanted me this much and those eyes tell me loud and clear that she doesn't just want my body. She doesn't just want me to satisfy this insatiable craving between her legs. She needs more—a lot more.

Can I go through with this? Am I even capable of that? I shouldn't try if I'm not. I shouldn't let her want me if I'm not capable of giving her everything she needs. She's already everything I need, but that doesn't matter.

I couldn't take her if I can't give her what she needs—everything she needs. I shouldn't make her think I even want to if I'm not going to go all the way and really be that to her.

"Lie down, baby. You need to rest."

I try to push her back on the mattress. She starts to comply and then realizes a split second later what I'm trying to do.

She throws her arms around my waist, presses her head into my stomach, and then cranes it back to look up at me all pleading and needy. "Don't.... Wes.... I need you.... please don't leave me......I need you...."

She rakes her hand up my chest, touches my cheek once the way she did that first morning we woke up together, and then looks back down at the floor. She huddles against my stomach and then, out of a distant haze, she moves her face down to my fly.

She rubs her cheek across my aching bulge once and then turns her mouth inward. She opens her mouth wide and closes it around my package just hard enough to tease me to raving insanity.

"I need you so bad...." she rasps. "Please.... please.... please...."

She jaws me again and again begging for it. The ache between my legs stabs upward into my stomach each time she says it. I can't take this. I can't do this. I can't let her do this.

"Don't, baby," I choke and clench my fingers in her hair. I have to stop her, but she won't stop.

She scrapes her teeth across my fly and sends another sizzling jet of heat stabbing through my whole being. She's so fucking hot that I'm starving for her, but I ......I love her so much.

That word comes to my mind without me even trying. I love her too much to let her sit here begging for me when she's already out of her mind from earlier.

My fingers tighten on her shoulders. I should push her off, but I find it impossible to break away from her mouth. I know what it will feel like. I want to explode in her mouth, but I don't want to treat her that way. I want to cherish her and protect her and care for her the way she needs me to.

She looks up at me with that same drunken, pained expression. Her face shines with desire and I almost collapse when she takes hold of my belt. I can only stand and stare in rapture as she tugs it loose.

I know exactly what's going to happen if she gets my pants open. I have to act now. I push her away and steer her up the mattress. "Get in bed, baby."

She doesn't fight me when I pull the covers down and then tuck her in. She keeps clawing at my arms when I arrange the blankets under her chin and comb her hair back on the pillow.

"Don't leave, Wes," she whines. "Please.... I need you here...."

"I know you do, baby."

"Please......don't leave me alone. Please.... stay......"

I know she needs me. She needs me here with her. I consider lying down on top of the bedspread fully clothed and then change my mind.

I walk around to the other side of the bed and she watches me take my clothes off. I'll just have to control myself once I get in bed with her and I can do that, now that I know what she needs.

She needs me to be gentle with her. I can love her. I can take her. I can fill her with pleasure and let her touch me, but I can't lose control with her. That's my job—to make sure she's all right.

I climb under the covers and she falls into my arms. She cowers against my chest and I stroke her hair. She means so much to me. I don't understand it, but it's real. I know that much.

I never want anything to happen to her, and as long as I'm here, I won't let it. I need to protect her from my own desires more than anything. I need to make sure my desire for her doesn't hurt her in any way.

She moves her arms and hands across my skin in the warm dark under the covers. She touches me and kisses me and I feel her rising desire infecting me, but it isn't the same as before. She doesn't spin me out of control. I can handle it now, and no matter what happens, I always will.

Chapter 18: Wes

I scroll through a missing persons list from Nashville, Tennessee, but I don't find what I'm looking for so I click back over to the coroner's report on the male victim found in the car trunk.

The guy was bald with greying brown hair and a mustache. No one on the Nashville list fits that description so I go to the next list on the page my buddy in Singapore sent over.

I scroll through that one, too, when an email notification comes up on my screen. It's from a homeless shelter in Utah and they don't have any record of the woman whose description I sent through.

That's another dead end in my decade-long search to find out who my parents were. I'll probably never find out. I keep investigating the case more out of habit than from any hope of finding anything.

I don't need to find anything. Finding my parents or even finding out who they were would add nothing to my life now. I don't even know why I keep investigating them. I guess that's the point. I've been doing it for so long that it's easier to just keep doing it than it would be to stop.

I switch back over to the coroner's report. I've already read it at least thirty times, but I go over it again searching for any missing detail. There has to be something here that I'm missing.

I prick up my ears when I hear footsteps crossing the bedroom floor in the room next door. Natalie comes into my home office dressed in my bathrobe that is miles too big for her. She squints into the light and her hair is a mess. "What are you doing in here? It's three-thirty in the morning."

"I couldn't sleep and I didn't want to wake you up. You should go back to bed, baby."

"I don't want to go back to bed if you're in here. I came over to be with you. If I wanted to sleep alone, I could do that at home." She crosses the room and rests her hand on my shoulder while she squints at the screen. "What are you working on?"

"The victims in the trunk of the car case." I put my arm around her waist and kiss her. "Would you be able to sleep if I came back to bed with you? Is that what you need? Do you want me to be with you while you sleep?"

"I don't want you to lie there awake while I sleep. If you can't sleep, you should work. Have you found out anything else about the victims?"

"No. That's what I was just doing." I frown up at her. "Are you really interested in this?"

"I'm interested in whatever you're interested in." She lets out a tremendous yawn. "Who's the email from?"

"It's something about my parents' case. Come here. If you aren't going back to bed, at least sit down."

I pull her onto my lap and she reclines sideways against my shoulder. She starts to nestle into me when she suddenly sits up. "Wes?"

"Yes?" I ask.

"Are you still investigating me?"

"No, I stopped when I found out the case had been sealed by a judge. There was nothing else to investigate."

"Aren't you.... don't you even want to know what happened?"

"Of course I want to know what happened."

"Why aren't you investigating it then?"

"I just told you. The court case was sealed. It's a dead end."

"Are you telling me you couldn't hack it and find out?"

I cock my head to study her. "I would rather find out from you. I would much rather know that you trusted me enough to tell me yourself. Besides, hacking the case wouldn't tell me what I really want to know."

"Which is what?"

"How it affected you. You told me at the barbecue that your dad's case had something to do with why you can't keep a boyfriend. Then, at the diner, you told me that your boyfriends didn't stick around because you were constantly helping people. There's obviously a disconnect there between one and the other and hacking your dad's case wouldn't tell me what that is. Only you can."

She looks away for a second and her features wrench. I'm touching a nerve here. I'm doing something much worse than that, but we were always going to have this conversation.

"Whatever your dad's case has to do with you, I need to know about it because it affects me now that I'm involved with you. If your dad's case is somehow stopping you from keeping a boyfriend, then I need to know what it is. I need to know how it might cause problems for us."

She gulps and her eyes glisten with aching emotion. "Are we involved? Are you my boyfriend?"

I have to smile. I love her. I know it, but I don't need to make it worse for her by telling her—not yet. I don't want to scare her.

"I don't know if I'm your boyfriend or something else, but whatever your dad's case did to you, I don't want the same thing to happen to us. I want us to last."

"You do?"

"Of course I do, baby. Did you think I didn't? Did you really think it was like this with the other women I dated? I would be married to one of them now if it was like this."

She stares at me with huge eyes. "Is that what you want—to marry me?"

"I didn't say that, but it was never like this before. I don't want anything to get in the way of this. I want to know what happened with your dad's case, but it's more important to me that you tell me yourself. I want you to tell me because you trust me and because you want me to know. I don't want to find out another way."

She looks away again thinking about it. "If we're involved, is that your way of having a family? Is that why you're doing this?"

I turn all the way around to look directly at her. "This isn't about me. I don't want you helping me and giving me what I need. This is about you and giving you the help you need. I want to be that to you. I want to be the one who gives you what you need when no one else does. I want to be the one you come to for the help you need and I want to be the one who takes care of you in ways no one else does."

She sits on my lap blinking while she takes that in. Now she knows, but I feel content saying it. Now all the cards are out on the table and she knows why I'm here.

She glances toward the computer and then curls into a ball on my lap. She leans back on my chest and tucks her head into my neck right against my shoulder. I put my arm around her, kiss her hair, pull her against me, and go back to checking the missing persons lists.

She watches for a minute and then softens. Her breathing lengthens and her body goes limp as she falls back to sleep.

I turn down the brightness on my screen and switch off the desk lamp to make the room darker. I keep my arm around her while I click on the mouse. Now we can both do what we need to do and I don't have to worry about her anymore.

Chapter 19: Natalie

I come out of the elevator to find Gina standing at the reception desk with Phil Ames, the Celestial Hotel's general manager.

An old man standing across the counter from them yells at them in full flight. He gesticulates wildly and waves his phone at them while all the other guests stand back and watch the unfolding catastrophe.

I go over to stand next to Gina. "What's going on?"

The old guy rounds on me. "I keep telling these people that I made this reservation six months ago! Now I show up here and they tell me they don't have a record of my reservation at all! I just came into town for my daughter's wedding and the whole bridal party is staying here! I show up here to check into my room and these people tell me I don't have a room reserved."

I turn to Gina. "What's the problem? Did he have a reservation?"

"It's right here!" he bellows and shoves his phone at me. "I have the confirmation email right here!"

I hold out my hand. "Do you mind if I take a look? We can get this figured out. I'm the Chief Operations Officer for the whole Triple Star chain. I promise we'll work this out one way or the other." I hold out my hand toward his phone. "Can I take a look?"

"Fine. You figure it out. It's your problem, not mine."

He shoves his phone into my hands and I look down at the confirmation email. "Oh. I understand what the problem is. You registered at the Celestial Parade Hotel in Miami by mistake."

"Well, what the hell good does that do me?!" he roars. "What the hell good does it do if I want to give my daughter away at the altar here when I'm staying in a hotel in Miami? You're the ones who messed this up. You fix it."

He snatches the phone out of my hand and I turn back to Phil and Gina. "We already explained that his daughter's wedding is taking up almost three whole floors of the building," Phil tells me. "We're booked solid because we've had to squash all our other guests into the other floors."

"What does that have to do with anything?" the guy bellows. "I'm not leaving this hotel until you give me a room!"

"We can give you a room at the Ebony Hotel," Phil goes on. "It's another Triple Star hotel right down the street. We would comp the room so it doesn't cost you anything. That's the best we can do."

"That isn't good enough!" the old man thunders. "I'm staying here with my daughter and the rest of the bridal party. I don't care what it takes. Throw out one of the other guests if you have to! I'm not leaving until you fix this."

I don't know what to say to him. My mind switches to the other floors of the building—the ones Triple Star uses as its corporate offices. I can't think of any of them that could be converted quickly into a hotel room, but what else is there?

At that moment, another guest comes forward from the back of the line. Sid Brownstone approaches the desk and slides over to my side.

I've known Sid for years. He's been coming here every other month on business. He's part of the Triple Star family and he treats most of the staff like he's their second father.

"I could move over to the Ebony Hotel," Sid offers. "I'm here on business so it doesn't really matter which hotel I stay in." He turns to the old man. "I'd be happy to stay there instead if it means you can give your daughter away."

"Thank you, Sid," I exclaim. "You're a lifesaver."

He grins at me, puts his arm around my shoulders, and gives me a quick hug. "How many times have you saved my backside over the years? It's the least I can do."

Phil bends over Gina's computer. "Sid is reserved for a week and the wedding is only five days. That's perfect. Thank you, Sid."

"It's a pleasure." Sid beams at the old man and shakes his hand. "Congratulations on your daughter's wedding. I hope she and her new husband are very happy."

"Thank you, Sid," I say again. "Phil will transfer your reservation over to the Ebony and we'll comp it for you. We really appreciate it."

"I'll be on my way, then. I'll see you folks when I come back to town two months from now." He takes hold of his suitcase, waves to us, and wheels his out of the lobby.

Phil goes to work on the computer making a thousand clicks. "You're all set, Sir. You're in room 245. That's right down the hall from your daughter." He hands the old man the keycode card to his room.

The old man frowns at him, at me, and then at the card in his hand. "That's it? It's all taken care of—just like that?"

"Just like that. Enjoy the wedding. Don't hesitate to let us know if you need anything else—anything at all."

The old guy wanders off to the elevator. "You're a genius, Nat," Gina murmurs in my ear. "None of that would have happened if you didn't make such a point of treating all the guests like family."

I'm just about to answer when my phone buzzes. "Are you guys all set? I gotta go."

"We're good," Phil replies. "Thanks, Nat."

I get back in the elevator still frowning at my phone. A text from Andy Ireland, the Triple Star CIO, stares back at me from the screen. *Get upstairs on the double. It's a matter of life and death.*

I text him back. *I'm on my way. What's going on?*

The shit is hitting the fan. Get up here now.

I don't know what to think, but I'm already in the elevator. I can't get up there any faster by running.

I step out on the top corporate floor. It looks quiet and peaceful except that all the people who usually work in the cubicles are all standing around whispering to each other.

I don't want to stop and gossip, but the tension in the air is explosive. I head for Andy's office and find the door standing open and Andy gone.

I turn away when I hear loud voices coming from another office down the hall from mine. It's coming from Ryan Koch's office. He's Triple Star's CEO and I find Andy and all the other executives crowded in there talking loud and fast.

I stand in the doorway watching, but I can't make out anything over the noise. The other execs crowd around Ryan shoving, yelling, and chopping the air. I can see from their blotchy, distorted faces that they're all furious....and scared.

Andy spots me and spins around fast. "Here! You explain this to Natalie! I can't wait to hear this! You stand here and tell her to her face what you just told me!"

Dead silence falls over the room and my gaze darts from one face to the next. I've known these people for years and I know them all like family.

They back away still glaring and curling their lips in disgust. Some of them won't even look at me, they're so irate.

Ryan stands in front of his desk and all the others part to make a clear path between him and me. "Well?!" Andy roars and waves back and forth between me and Ryan. "Tell her! Let us hear you explain this to her. I would love to hear you try!"

"What's going on?" I don't want to know. "What's the problem?"

Ryan wipes his hand across his mouth, sweeps back his jacket on both sides to prop his hands on his hips, and looks away.

"You better start talking or I will!" Andy yells and then turns to me. "They bought us out! They went behind our backs and bought us out overnight! We're fucked, Nat! We're totally, one hundred percent fucked!"

My stomach drops. "Who bought us out?"

"Monarch Resorts Group," Ryan murmurs. "They pulled a hostile takeover on us overnight. They couldn't stop us from taking the Summit Hotel, so they got it this way."

"That bastard Winslow did this," Andy snarls. "He's a shark. This is exactly the kind of bullshit move he would pull."

My blood runs cold. Wes......He couldn't do this to me. He couldn't take Triple Star away from me.

"It gets worse," Maya Butcher, our CFO, adds. "They're sending their own HR team over here tomorrow and they're going to start cleaning house."

"Well, I'm not waiting." Andy turns away and storms toward the door. "I won't wait around for them to fire me. I'm leaving now. I've given Triple Star the best years of my life. No way in hell am I working for Monarch. I put up with enough of that cutthroat, gladiator-style management with Bill Simons. I'll be damned if I do it again."

He slams the door behind him and the rest of the executives look back and forth at each other. I can't believe this. Wes couldn't do this to me. He couldn't pretend to value what Triple Star stands for and then gut me behind my back.

I can't believe it, but Ryan reads my mind. He picks up a folder from his desk and hands it to me. I flip it open and there are the documents staring back in my face.

Wes. He talked a good line, but when it all came down to it, it was all business. Nothing else matters to him. He'll do anything to get what he wants. I should have seen this coming. That just goes to show how naïve I really am that I believed he would ever be any different.

Chapter 20: Wes

I move a stack of papers to the other side of my desk and cock my ear when I hear voices yelling outside my office door. "You can't go in there, Ma'am! You can't go in there......!"

The door blasts off its hinges and Natalie barges in. My EA Melissa flutters around her waving in Natalie's face. "You can't come in here, Ma'am. I'm sorry but...."

Natalie shoves Melissa out of the way so hard she almost knocks Melissa off her feet. Natalie stomps over to my desk and yells at me across it. "How the hell do you have the balls to show your face in public after what you just did? How do you live with yourself after you just destroyed the organization I dedicated my whole life to? Are you that rotten that you could go behind our backs and buy us out...and now you want to tear the whole thing apart and turn it into another factory farm just like every other Monarch business? What the fuck is wrong with you?"

"I didn't know anything about the hostile takeover," I tell her. "I only found out about it this morning and I've been doing damage control all day. I swear to you, Natalie. The Board of Directors did this without my knowledge. They knew I'd oppose it so they engaged another firm to affect the takeover behind my back. They fucked me over the same as you and they just sprang it on me a few hours ago. I swear it. I would never do something like this to you or to Triple Star."

She stands there fuming, but at least she heard me. "I don't believe you. You're the CEO of the whole company. You build this company from one restaurant. You could have stopped them."

I get ready for another assault to explain it to her when Angie Crouch comes into my office and holds out another stack of documents. "The Board of Directors is calling you upstairs, Sir. They say it's urgent."

"I'm on my way. You can go back to work, Melissa. I'll handle this."

She shoots Natalie an uncertain glance and then leaves. I walk around my desk and lower my voice when I get near Natalie. She still glares at me, but at least she doesn't recoil at my approach.

"I already pulled out all the stops trying to reverse the takeover, but the board had already purchased enough shares of Triple Star stock before I found out. It's too late and they told me that if I don't cooperate, they'll force me out and replace me as CEO. The only way I can help you is by staying here and working with them. I'm sorry. I'm already doing everything I can to help Triple Star. Believe me." I swallow hard. "Please believe me. I would never do this to you."

She glances up at me and then turns away with a sickening grimace. "I can't believe this. Everyone at Triple Star thinks you did it."

"I didn't. I wouldn't." I lower my voice even further. "You mean too much to me. I would never do anything to threaten what we have and I know what Triple Star means to you. Please look at me and tell me you believe me."

She meets my gaze for a fraction of an instant and looks away again. She barely croaks above a whisper. "I believe you."

"I have to go. I'll call you later when I know something."

She doesn't move and she keeps her head turned. "You know what this means, don't you? It means.... you're my boss. We can't be involved anymore."

"I know." I run my fingertip down her cheek and let my hand fall. I can't do any more than that. She's my subordinate now. Whatever we had ends today.

I quickly pull her head toward me, kiss her hair, and walk out of the office. I can't stay in the same room with her a second longer without doing something inappropriate.... or quitting.

That was the last kiss. We'll never have anything else to do with each other outside a professional capacity.

Now it's up to me to preserve as much of Triple Star as I can. I have to do it for her. I have to make sure all her hard work doesn't come to nothing.

I go upstairs to find the Board of Directors, the rest of Monarch's executives, and most of the company's general managers assembled in the boardroom.

I go over to Richard Hurt, the Chairman of the Board. He holds out his hand to me. "Thank you for coming."

"Sure," I reply. "What's up?"

"We're just discussing the HR situation. Walter here has been going over the employee records for Triple Star starting with the executive suite. It turns out that almost none of the executives and top management staff have any relevant qualifications for doing their jobs. Hardly any of them have any formal education or industry training."

"They have the qualifications and experience of running the company effectively for years," I point out. "If they can do that without formal education, what difference does it make?"

"Monarch doesn't work that way. You know that. We only hire the best. We're sending over a company-wide memo this afternoon requiring all staff from the top to the bottom to reapply for their positions. Every position in the company will be posted on the open market and anyone will be able to apply and compete for these jobs. We want to make sure we get the best people in these positions."

I open my mouth to point out that this won't work with a company like Triple Star, but Richard is already turning to Walter. "We'll need to do a full audit on the backgrounds of all employees to make sure they comply with Monarch's morals clause."

"Of course," Walter replies. "I'd expect nothing less."

I swallow down a wave of nausea, but I can't leave without risking my position. I have to stay here. I have to do something to help Triple Star. I owe it to Natalie, at least.

I catch my CFO, Jim Kaufman, looking at me across the boardroom. He was with me during the Summit negotiation. He knows exactly what HR will find when they start digging into Triple Star's employee records. I can just imagine the carnage when that happens.

Chapter 21:
Natalie

I walk into the lobby at the Celestial Hotel, but I have to stop on the threshold. I can't get into the building with hundreds of employees packed to the walls.

Shouting and scuffling comes from the other end of the lobby near the elevators, but I can't see over all the heads and bodies in my way. "What's going on?" I ask those nearest me.

"The HR people from Monarch are here," one of the bellboys tells me. "They're reading us the riot act about how things are gonna change around here. It ain't going down too well."

I can't listen to this. I push my way into the crowd. "Let me through. Excuse me. Let me through."

A ripple of tension goes through the people surrounding me and calls radiate outward from my position. "Nat's here! Let her through! Natalie's coming through!"

The crowd squeezes apart on both sides and I wedge my way toward the elevators.

I smash myself between Baner, Rocker, Petey, and Fernando to see a bunch of strangers in suits standing in front of the elevator. A man raises both hands and tries to talk over the noise of hundreds of employees all yelling back at him.

The restaurant staff, the cleaning crew, and every other department are all here. They stand in groups scowling and bellowing at these strangers. These people must be the Monarch HR staff.

The employees are all too furious to notice me, and as soon as I show up, Harvey Joiner from the North Star steps up on a bench by the elevators. He raises his arms the same way and the other employees settle down immediately.

"We all know why we're here!" he yells over the crowd. "We've given Triple Star our blood, sweat, and tears for years. Some of us have been here since the beginning and we've helped turn this company around so it's the best place in the world to work. WE did that! We made this company a success when its finances were in the toilet. We did that by taking care of each other and making each other the most important people in the world to each other."

Cheers break out and a surge of bodies almost sweeps me off my feet. People raise their fists and yell back at Harvey.

He raises his arms again and everyone falls silent to listen to him. "Now these strangers want to come in and raze all our hard work to the ground. They want to turn Triple Star back into the nightmare it was before WE took over. They want to undo all our hard work, tear us apart, and turn us against each other. Well, I WON'T LET THEM!! I didn't pour my heart and soul into this company to watch some strangers flush it all down the toilet! I'm walking out right now and I want all of you to come with me. They can't run this place without us. Triple Star is my family, and if someone comes along and takes that away from me, then THERE IS NO TRIPLE STAR!! If I can't have Triple Star, THEY CAN'T, EITHER!!"

The yelling, bellowing, and cheering rise to a deafening pitch. I really need to plug my ears, but I can't raise my arms with Rocker, Fernando, and Baner crushing me from all sides.

Harvey pulls a hammer from his pocket and points it out over the crowd. "Come on! Let's go! We're walking out! We're leaving this shithole! WHO'S WITH ME?!!"

An answering wave of noise echoes through the lobby and the mob surges back the other way. The crush around me lessens slightly and then all the laundry guys turn away as the employees pour through the entrance doors on their way outside.

They hug each other and a few shed tears before they all walk away in different directions. Charlotte comes over to me and hugs me. "Thank you for everything, Natalie. I love you. Call me, okay? We'll make it through this."

"I know, sweetie. Take care of yourself."

I hug her and then watch the rest of the employees leave until Tommy comes over to me. "Are you coming, Nat? Come with us."

"I might. I need to go see what's happening upstairs. I want to make sure there's no way to salvage this."

"There isn't." He shoots a dangerous scowl past my shoulder and lowers his voice to a hiss. "They're upstairs going through everyone's records to see if anyone violates Monarch's morals clause. You know what that means."

He hugs me and leaves. The lobby completely empties until I'm the only one left. The lobby, the front desk, the restaurant, and every other department of the hotel lie desolate, abandoned, and ghostly.

I turn around very slowly. I've never seen the Celestial like this—or any other hotel for that matter. Not even Bill Simons could wreak such destruction on the company I love. I can just imagine what's going on in the rest of Triple Star's hotels.... or it will be once word gets out.

The Monarch HR people stand in front of the elevator. Some of them look stricken while others frown at the empty hotel like they really don't understand what the hell just happened.

"You could have stopped them, Ms. Fahey," one guy says. "You *should* have stopped them. We can't run the hotel without the staff."

I snort and push between them to hit the elevator button. "Good luck with that. You're the HR people here. You go manage your human resources and let me know how that works out for you. See if you can convince them to come back and care about Monarch the way they've been caring about Triple Star all these years."

"You're the COO and you work for Monarch now," a woman chimes in. "You owe it to Monarch to do your best to keep these hotels running."

"Those people who just walked out are my family. You aren't. I don't owe you or Monarch jack shit. Wes Winslow told me in his own words that Monarch values distancing yourselves from the people who work under you. You want to view your service people as less than yourselves, so go on and do it. You all belong to HR which means you're subordinate to me. Go do your jobs and don't come crying to me if your methods don't work."

The elevator opens and I step inside. The HR people gape at me like I'm speaking another language, but I really don't give a shit anymore. Harvey is right. There is no Triple Star anymore.

Triple Star was people helping people. Triple Star was family and now that's gone. What's the point of running a business without the people, both the employees and the guests? A business is no good without those connections.

I ride up the elevator to find the top floor in a state of desolation and disaster. All the cubicles stand empty and more loud voices come from Ryan's office.

I go straight there dreading what I'll find. I freeze when I walk in on the Triple Star executive committee, a bunch of new strangers I've never laid eyes on, and the Monarch executive committee, including Wes.

He stands off to one side and doesn't say anything while the strangers rage against the Triple Star executives. I figure out pretty quick that these strangers are the Monarch Resorts Group Board of Directors—the same people who did this to us in the first place.

One guy roars in Ryan's face. "How dare you pull a stunt like this! You're obligated by your company charter to run your operation to the best of your ability no matter who the shareholders are! The takeover shouldn't make any difference! If you can't control your employees, what choice do we have but to bring in our own managers to do the job for you?"

"I already told you!" Ryan yells back. "It was your HR people who did this! Do you honestly think you can change our culture overnight and the employees will just lie down and let you walk all over them? These are human beings! They can decide for themselves who they work for! They aren't your slaves! When are you gonna get that?"

"I don't believe you didn't have something to do with this," the guy counters. "We're seeing entire hotels emptied across the whole chain. Nearly every employee in the entire company has walked off the job."

The deputy who helped Wes during the Summit negotiation spots me. "Ms. Fahey! Everyone listens to you. You can convince the employees to come back."

Everyone else turns around to stare at me and the guy that was just yelling at Ryan comes over to extend his hand to me. "Ms. Fahey! We've heard a lot about you. I'm Richard Hurt, Chairman of Monarch's Board of Directors."

I look down at his hand and sniff. "I hope you're happy. You bought us out. You can spend the rest of your career dreaming about matching the profits we've enjoyed because you just pissed all that down the drain."

"You must be able to do something about this. You're respected by all the staff. They listen to you. You can convince them to come under Monarch's umbrella."

"I don't think so. This company's culture is the main reason these people keep working here and I feel the same way. I'm considering quitting myself."

A few people gasp behind his back. Are they Monarch people or Triple Star people?

None of the Triple Star people try to talk me out of it. Of course not.

"I hope you'll reconsider, Ms. Fahey," Hurt goes on. "We value your work. We would hate to lose your talent."

"Are you sure about that? I hear you're looking into the employees' backgrounds. You might find something in my record that violates your morals clause."

He bursts out laughing. "I doubt that...." His smile evaporates when he sees my expression. "You aren't serious!"

"I don't have any secondary education. I don't have any formal business training at all. I learned how to run this company by working my way up from the front desk. Are you sure you can't find someone else better to take my place?" I scan the people in the room. "Which one of you is the COO?"

A young guy standing near Wes raises his hand. "That's me, Ma'am. I'm Mike Reed, but I just took over a few weeks ago. I'm sure you're way better than me and I could learn a lot from you. I hope we can work together."

He seems nice, but the next second, Richard Hurt draws my attention back to himself. "We'll keep Triple Star insulated from the rest of Monarch for the time being. We'll leave the executive committee in place and you'll all keep running this company as you were until we can affect a smooth transfer."

"Why are your HR people making decisions about our employees, then?" I ask.

"That's just standard procedure for all Monarch acquisitions. It's nothing personal."

"Everything at Triple Star is personal. If your HR people are pissing off our employees, then we aren't insulated, are we?"

"Well, we couldn't have anyone working for us, even in an insulated capacity, that violates our morals clause. That's just basic business practice."

"Then you're out of luck. You get your HR people to run this hotel and see what happens to your profits. I'll be in my office if you want me to do anything, but without any employees, it looks like I won't have much to do for quite a while.... or at least until your HR people hire a whole new staff."

I turn away to walk out of the room. "Ms. Fahey!" he calls after me. "You'll need to reapply for your position just like the rest of the staff. We'll need to evaluate your qualifications to ensure we have the right person for the job."

"I won't reapply. If you want me to do this job, that's your business. Otherwise, I'm sure I can get another job working the front desk at some other hotel."

Chapter 22: Wes

I knock on Natalie's apartment door and shuffle my feet while I wait for her to answer. I've only been here once before when I picked her up for our date—our only date and probably our last.

I probably shouldn't be here, but I need to see her. My life is falling apart ever since the Triple Star takeover.

She pulls the door open and shoots me a fierce look before she slumps when she sees that it's me. "You shouldn't be here."

"I know. I just needed to see you."

She walks off into her apartment, but she leaves the door open for me to follow her inside. Her apartment is big, spacious, modern, and spotless with massive windows looking out over the city.

She sits on a stool at the kitchen counter and taps on her phone. "What can I do for you? I would offer you a drink, but that would imply that I want you to stick around, which I don't."

"I don't want you to do anything for me. I came to see how you're doing...you and your employees."

"They aren't my employees anymore, but since you ask, they're doing okay. We're pulling together to help each other through this and help each other find jobs."

"Does that mean you're helping them find jobs?"

She shoots me a look, but a hint of a smile sneaks into it. "That isn't really your concern anymore. You're working for the other side."

"I'm sorry about this."

"You want me to believe you had nothing to do with this, so you have nothing to be sorry about. It's the Board of Directors I can't forgive, but fortunately, they'll get their payback once their profits go down the toilet. They're already dealing with mass employee walkouts and now the guests are rebelling, too."

"What do you mean?"

"The guests are canceling their reservations by the dozen. The Board of Directors can bring in a bunch of Monarch employees to run our hotels, but our guests don't want to be served by strangers. They're canceling, and since our loyal returning guests are the heart of our business, Triple Star's profits will never return to the level they were before. The stock share price has already tanked. The Board of Directors will never recoup the money they spent to buy us out."

"And you're happy about that, aren't you?" I ask. "You're happy the Board of Directors is going to get payback for this. You should be happy about it."

"I'm not happy about it. I liked Triple Star the way it was before. I'm as upset as everyone else that it's dead now."

"You don't look upset. You're still at work. You're still running the company on our behalf. I thought you would have quit by now."

She finally raises her eyes to meet mine and she winces. "I wish I could. I really do."

"You could. What's stopping you?"

She shrugs, but at that moment, her phone rings. She answers it and starts having a conversation with someone on the other end. "Hi. Thanks. Yes. Wednesday at 10 AM would be perfect. Thank you. Is there anything I need to bring? Did you get the medical records I sent over? Okay. I'll call my old doctor and remind them to send them over. Can you still do it without the records? Okay. I'll follow up and make sure you get them in time. Thanks."

She hangs up and puts her phone down.

"What was that about?" I ask. "Why do you have a medical appointment? Is anything wrong?"

"Nothing's wrong. I got pregnant that first night we hooked up, but don't worry about it. I'm taking care of it."

I blink trying to put my world back on its axis. "You're what? You said you were on birth control."

"I am. I use the ring, but I guess...." She turns bright red, waves her hand, and hops off the stool. She paces around the kitchen not looking at me. "I guess.... you're a lot bigger than any guy I've ever been with before. I guess the ring got knocked out of place. Anyway, it doesn't matter. I'm going in next week and we won't have to think about it again."

I stare at her trying to get my brain working. "You're.... pregnant?"

"Not for very much longer. Don't worry about it."

This energy building in me won't let me stand here gawking at her like a fool. I stride down the long windows looking out at nothing. She's pregnant?

What the hell is happening to me? I've been through this with other women, but she......

I can't think. None of my brain cells want to connect with any others. Nothing makes sense, especially not the thoughts going through my head right now.

Everything she's been showing me and telling me for weeks comes together, but it doesn't make any sense.

She sits back down on the stool and does something on her phone. I can't look at her, but she's still there in my head. She'll always be in my head.

She came into my life and turned everything upside down. Now I'm looking at the world in reverse from the way it looked just a few weeks ago.

Everything I thought was good now seems bad. Everything I once thought was bad now seems good. I don't know how to live in this upside-down world.

I walk away toward the door. I need to get away from her. She doesn't say anything when I walk outside and head for my car, but I can't drive anywhere. None of this makes sense.

She's pregnant. With my child. My child. I'm a father.

Pictures flood my mind along with a torrential avalanche of confused emotions. I used to see those pictures all the time when I was younger. I saw kids playing around and adults.... a man....

I spent years of my childhood dreaming that someone would come for me. I thought they were just out of sight.... that maybe they got lost or held up or that they just couldn't find me. I thought they would come back for me as soon as they realized where I was.

I counted the days until they came back and took me......home.... home to the place with the kids playing....and him......that man....my father.

There was a woman there, too. She smiled at the kids playing in the sunshine. She smiled at the man, too. All those feelings.... all those pictures......

Am I the child or the man? I'm both. I'm in both places feeling.... everything.... all the pain, all the joy, all the sorrow.... it's all in there mixed up in this jumbled soup.

That's why I started investigating them—to try to find them. I thought if they only knew where I was, how much I wanted them, that they would come.

Are they still out there waiting for me? Are they still aching and yearning for me the same way I ache and yearn for them? Can they still take me home?

I haven't thought about or remembered any of that for years. I put it away in a dark corner of my being where I didn't have to see it or feel it or know it anymore. I told myself I didn't care, but it was all still there. It was just waiting....

It was waiting for me to come and find it. That child is waiting for me to come and take them home. I can't let them go through what I went through. I can't let them wait there year after year wondering where I am.

I make it five blocks before something clicks in my mind. I spin around, storm back to her apartment, and walk in without knocking. She's still sitting on the stool messing with her phone.

"Don't get rid of it, Natalie, please," I blurt out in a rush. "Don't get rid of it. Keep it. We can do this. I have to. I need this. I don't know what I'll do or how I'll do it, but I have to. Don't do anything. Just have the baby. I need you to. Please. I'll do anything. Just don't get rid of it."

"I have to." She bends over her phone like I just asked her not to order Chinese food.

I turn away to leave, but all those pictures come crashing back into my head. I feel them slipping through my fingers and I grasp at them to hold onto them.

I need to keep seeing those kids running around in the yard......the man......the woman......

That aching feeling of.... going home. It's out there somewhere. They're still out there somewhere waiting for me. I just need to find them.

I take five steps before I come back. I want to scream, not at her, but at myself. "Don't do this. You don't have to. I'll take care of it. I'll take care of you. I have to. Don't you see? This baby.... this baby is the only family I'm ever gonna have. Don't take that away from me......"

I can't hold back and my voice breaks. My throat hurts. I don't know half of what I'm saying. I shouldn't do this, but I can't go back. There is no going back for me anymore.

I turn my back on her pressing my wrist to my mouth. I can't break down in front of her. She already said she was going to do this.

My whole being revolts against this. I keep floundering for a way to make it not true. She can't cut me off like this just when I found.... I don't know what I found. I don't even know what this is.

I take a long time to compose myself enough to face her. When I do, she sits up straight on her stool and her face looks just as devastated as I feel. I've never seen her this hurt, not even when she confronted me about the takeover.

"I can't," she husks. "I'm sorry. I wish I could, but I can't."

Those words tear my heart to shreds, mostly because of her expression and the broken misery in her tone when she says it. She feels the same way I do, but she can't.

My whole soul screams and shrieks at her not to do this, but I can't let that out. I couldn't do that to her.

The pictures start running through my fingers again and I panic trying to hold onto them. I can't let them slip away. They'll take my whole life with them. I'll die without them.

I would never stop searching for that child. I would never rest until I found them and took them home. I don't even know where home is. Where is the child? I would scour the whole world, every day, every hour. I would die yearning for them.

If they ever searched for me, they would discover that I died trying to find them. Then at least they would realize how much I love them.

I can't survive this devouring love for....my child. It's right there in front of me, right there inside her body....and yet, I can't find it. I can't reach it. I can't save it. My heart bleeds praying to God I can somehow reach it before it slips away entirely.... but I can't.

She already said she can't keep it. If she goes through with this, I'll be lost. I'll never get it back. It will be gone forever—gone somewhere I can never find it. Will I still be a father then? Will I still be the man in the field?

I'll always be a father. I'm a father now. I'll always love that child. I'll love it more than my own life.

What can I say to her? I can't explain any of that. She just said she can't keep it. I could never force that on her, but......

I made her a promise. I promised this would be about her, about helping her, about being there for her, about giving her the help she needs that she can't get from anyone else. What happened to that?

I bow my head struggling to hold back the tide. It will break me any second now. I can't look at her without losing it.

If I break down right here in front of her, she'll think she has to help me. She'll think she has to do something to make it okay for me. I can't do that to her. She's already working around the clock to make it okay for everyone else.

Maybe that's why she can't keep the child. She already has too many other people depending on her. She can't let them down by keeping something for herself.

I can't ask that. I can't ask for anything.

"I........" I can barely make myself heard, my throat hurts so bad. I have to keep stopping and starting. Her unbreakable stare leaves me nowhere to hide.

I stand before her broken and beaten. If she doesn't know by now how much this hurts, I can't tell her.

"I.... At least......" I swallow hard and force the words out. "At least.... let me drive you....to the appointment."

I keep my eyes on the floor, but the legs of her stool are already blurring in tears. There. I said it. I can't be anything to her but a hindrance—a reminder of the inconvenience this is causing her.

At least I can do this much. I can do the one thing she needs before I vanish out of her life forever.

"All right," she rasps back. "Ten o'clock Wednesday."

That's it. I walk out of her apartment as fast as I can. I don't dare to look at her or anything else until I get out to my car. Only then, in the privacy of the passenger compartment, do I cover my face and break down completely.

Chapter 23:
Natalie

I step into the Monarch Board of Directors boardroom and pause there to take in the scene. The Board of Directors sits on one side of their table with the Monarch executive committee on the other.

Wes sits with them, but he doesn't look at me. Looking at him hurts. If I ever doubted the sincerity of everything he said to me in my apartment, I only have to look at his face to realize how much this hurt him.

He never looks at me anymore, but every time I see him at work, it gets worse. He goes through the motions of his life even more robotically than before. He speaks in a lifeless, mumble. I can't tell if he ever looks at anyone, but he takes special pains never to make eye contact with me.

I'm not involved with Monarch's executive business so no one says anything to me about his change in behavior. They must be able to tell, though. The change is so dramatic. It's excruciating.

Every spark of vitality he once had disappeared in my apartment. He's dead now. He's a lurching, brainless zombie staggering through life. He has nothing left—no energy, no momentum. God only knows what he does with his time. He obviously doesn't care about anything.

I gulp at the sight of him. This baby was his only lifeline. It was his one chance and he lost that. He can never come back from this. I'm not even sure anymore if he wants to.

He never talks to me. He avoids all contact with me, and when circumstances like this force us to be in the same room, he doesn't look at me. He pretends I don't exist.

I can't blame him. No one knows better than I do what this baby means to him. I never dreamed he would realize so quickly what being a father would do for him, but he did. He got it instantly.

Now he'll never have that. He's losing everything if he hasn't lost it already. Can I really do that to him? I have to. I have to save myself first. I can't let this destroy me which is what would happen if I kept this baby.

Richard Hurt startles me back to reality. "Come on in, Ms. Fahey. Take a seat."

I tear my attention away from Wes. There has to be a way to help him. There has to be a way to bring him back from the brink, but the only way to do that is to have the baby and I'm not going to do that. I couldn't throw my whole life away on that.

I face the Board of Directors and brace myself for a fight. Dealing with these people is always a fight.

They've kept their word about keeping Triple Star insulated from the rest of Monarch—except for HR. Mike Reed has been really nice. In fact, all the executives have been really nice. Most of them were at the Summit negotiation, so they know what Triple Star stands for.

Too bad they're all subordinate to the Board of Directors so the executives' hands are just as tied as mine.

I sit down across from Richard and he kicks things off in his usual jocular tone that sets my teeth on edge. "Well, Ms. Fahey, it appears that the Monarch employees we brought in to run the Celestial and all of Triple Star's other properties are working out pretty well. All the Triple Star hotels are back up and running."

"Yeah. You're right," I reply. "The Monarch people are as good as they can be under the circumstances."

He plows right on ahead as if I didn't say anything. Why do I bother?

"Reservations are still down, though. Nearly all of Triple Star's reservations have been canceled and only a trickle of new ones are coming in."

I nod. "That's understandable."

"Why is it understandable?" one of the other directors asks. "Are you and the former employees waging some kind of boycott against us? Did you incite the guests to cancel their reservations?"

I try not to roll my eyes in annoyance, but a second later, I realize what I'm doing and go ahead and let it rip. Why should I spare their feelings?

"How many different ways do I have to say it? Triple Star's whole business model is based on intimate personal relationships between guests and staff. Guests come to us to interact with the staff they know and like—the staff they've been interacting with for years. The only new reservations you're getting are from new guests who have never stayed with us before. Don't you get it? It's no wonder the old guests don't want to come back."

"Are you saying you didn't contact your old guests to tell them not to stay with us anymore?"

"Of course I didn't!" I snap. "None of us did! We didn't have to. Weren't you paying attention? Most of the cancelations happened when the guests actually showed up at the front desk and realized what was happening. They arrived to stay with the people they know and love and they found a bunch of strangers in their places. What did you think was going to happen? I told you that you would never get the best out of your staff or your guests doing it this way, but you didn't listen."

Richard frowns. "When did you tell us that?"

Jim Kaufman, the CFO, raises his hand. "Um.... excuse me......She said it during the Summit negotiation so no one on the Board of Directors was there. Only the executive committee was there."

I glance over at him and spot Wes staring at the tabletop. The sight of him wakes me back up to what I'm doing here.

"Well, I'm saying it now. We don't run our business this way and we *won't* run our business this way. If you want to convert Triple Star to a Monarch business and run it along Monarch lines, you'll have to start with an entirely new customer base. You won't ever get those guests back."

"That's what we want you to do," Richard tells me. "We want you to convert Triple Star into a Monarch business and switch it all over to our way of doing things."

"How exactly do you want me to do that?" I ask.

"We want you to train new employees to the company values, hire to the company standards, and implement our system in all of Triple Star's hotels."

"I'm sorry," I reply, "but I won't do that."

His head snaps up. "Why not? That's your job as COO."

"Not anymore." I stand up and drop a sheet of paper on his desk. "I'm resigning as COO of Triple Star."

The executive committee gasps. The Board of Directors gapes at me with their mouths open.

Wes doesn't look up or show any sign of emotion or reaction at all. If he's half the man I think he is, he must have been expecting this a long time ago. He's probably just surprised I didn't quit sooner. I sure am.

"You don't have to do this, Ms. Fahey," Richard tells me.

"I don't have to do it. I'm doing it because I want to. I never wanted to work for Monarch and I don't want to work for Monarch now. I don't believe in your company values and I definitely won't train anyone to follow them. Your business model is flawed and you'll never be as profitable as you could be if you keep using it. Have a nice day."

I walk out of the room. I feel happier, now that I don't work for this rotten organization anymore. Now I just need to find another job.

I head out of the building, but I have to stop at HR and deliver another letter of resignation to them. I come out of the department and stand in front of the elevator thinking things over. My people from Triple Star will be thrilled when they hear that I quit. I don't have to worry about that.

I still feel the sting of it, though. I enjoyed my time at Triple Star. I don't want it to end, but it's already over. It's time to move on.

The elevator dings and I step inside, but right before the doors close, Wes darts into the car with me. The doors shut with both of us alone on the inside.

I turn to look up at him. The first words on my lips are to ask if he's okay, but I can see that he isn't. He'll never be okay again.

He doesn't have the same problem. He looks down at me with dull, dead, emotionless eyes. "Are you okay?"

"Yeah. I'm okay. I'm......sorry."

"Don't be. This is the right thing for you. You don't belong here. You were never going to work for Monarch. I'm only surprised you stuck around as long as you did."

"I'm not talking about that. I'm talking about you. I'm....so sorry.... for doing this to you."

He looks back down at the floor. His mouth says, "It isn't your fault," but it is. I did this to him. I ruined him.

"I didn't quit because of what happened with Triple Star." My throat hurts and my voice trembles. "I had to quit. I can't stay here seeing you like this...."

I break off and tears spring to my eyes.

He won't look at me. "Don't worry about me. I'll be all right."

I shake my head, but I'm too upset to speak. He won't be all right. I would do anything to help him—anything but the one thing I know *will* help him.

I can't even point out that we're no longer superior and subordinate. I don't work for him anymore. We could get back together.... but we can't. We'll never get back together—ever. It's all over. It's dead and gone and done.

Seeing him hurts too much. It's a constant slap in the face of what could be.

The elevator dings on the ground floor. The doors open. It's time for me to leave. I turn around to face him, but he doesn't look up. He keeps his eyes down.

"I'll see you Wednesday," I tell him.

He nods. "See you Wednesday.

I step out and the doors shut between us. That's it. It's over.

Chapter 24: Wes

I knock on Natalie's apartment door and force myself to make eye contact with her just once when she opens it. "Are you ready to go?" I ask.

"Yeah. I'm ready."

She follows me outside and I open the passenger door mechanically to let her get into my car. I don't look at her on my way across town. I don't know if she looks at me. It doesn't matter.

I park outside the family health clinic twenty minutes before ten. I can't look at her, so I look at the building across the street. "Are you sure you want to do this?"

"I have to." Her voice trembles. "I wish I didn't, but I do."

I take a deep, shuddering breath, but it does nothing to steady my nerves. I have to say this now. I won't get another chance.

"I don't expect you to do this for me. I won't ask that again and I don't want you to do it for me, but maybe you can do it for yourself. Maybe it's the one thing you really need—someone who will be your family and who will be there for you when you get home at the end of the day. Maybe you need to just let all these people live their own lives and handle their own problems while you take care of the one person who really needs you—the one person who will love you and be there for you—the one person who will make sure that you're never alone again."

"I can't!" she chokes. "I really wish I could. I would give anything for that! I really would, but I can't! I'm sorry!"

I glance over at her, and once I start, I can't look away. Her terrified eyes skip around the parking lot in frantic circles.

"You know you need this," I tell her. "You know you need a family of your own—not everyone else's. These people don't need you, but your baby does. You need this baby as much as it needs you. That's what a real family is—not all these people. They already have families. They don't need you. Why can't you give yourself the one thing you really need?"

"I can't!" Tears streak down her cheeks and her voice cracks with agonizing sobs. "I have to do this! I don't want to, but I have to."

"Why?" I ask. "Why would you do this if you don't want to? If you want this baby so bad and you wish you could, why can't you?"

"I can't!" she shrieks and then breaks down in sobs. "I'm sorry, Wes! I'm so sorry."

She bows over her lap with tears falling onto her hands. She doesn't look at me.

"Why, baby?" I want to cry from looking at her. "Why can't you?"

"My dad......"

I freeze. "What about him? What does he have to do with this?"

Her eyes make another circuit of the parking lot as tears stream down her cheeks. "My dad......had a friend......"

I can't move. I want to run away, but I can't.

"They were friends......from when they were little boys.... They went into business together when they were in high school.... They loved each other like brothers......"

I can't let her do this alone. I grab her hand and she doesn't let go. She doesn't stop me from being there for her and she starts talking faster in a desperate rush.

"We called him Uncle Richie. He was in and out of our house every day and we all loved him. He was like our second dad......except......he liked kids......He loved them."

She looks away toward the clinic. She won't turn again where I can see her.

"It started when I was five. He told me he loved me. He said he was the only man in my life. When I hit puberty, he got mad if he ever thought I was interested in a boy. He made me think I had to be loyal to him by never being with anyone else. I thought.... He made me think we were forever......I didn't know.... I didn't think......It was all I ever knew how to do......"

I swallow hard trying not to puke. "Are you saying.... Did you do with me what you did with him? Are you saying I reminded you of him? Is that why you......?"

"No! Never!" she shrieks and shoots me a terrible, gut-wrenching glance before she looks away. "He took what he wanted. He never let me do anything. He just did what he wanted and told me I loved it because he was the one and because I was his. He told me I loved it because I loved him. I.... I didn't know how to think......I just.... You.... You always let me do it myself. You made me do it myself. You let me show you what I wanted and how I wanted it. You always let me feel safe...."

She breaks down crying hard. Her whole body racks with sobs. I can't stand watching her, but I can't move a muscle, either. Hearing this is as hard as it is for her to say it.

"When I was fourteen, he came over when only I was there. He took me in my room and we were.... we were doing it....and my dad walked in on us. He saw what was going on and he went ballistic. He tried to attack Uncle Richie and Uncle Richie grabbed me and shoved me between himself and my dad. Uncle Richie held a knife to my throat and told my dad to back off. I was scared out of my mind....and then my dad pulled a gun and shot Uncle Ritchie in the head. I....... I didn't know what to think....... I thought me and Uncle Ritchie were forever.... I thought I'd never love anyone ever again......I thought my life was over...."

She collapses again and I can't hold back from touching her. I put my hand on her shoulder and then slide it to her back. She completely falls apart in the seat crying into her hands.

All of a sudden, she rockets upright, throws back her head, grits her teeth for the last assault, and glares through the front windshield. "A month later when my dad was in jail for murder, my mom found out I was pregnant and she took me to end it. I didn't want to, but she told me I had to. She said having Uncle Richie's kid would ruin my life. She said my whole future would be destroyed if I kept it. She said I would live the rest of my life with the reminder of him right in front of me and no kid should have to live with that hanging over their head and the kid's father was never going to be in its life anyway. I just wanted......"

She dissolves in tears and her voice strains to a high, squeaky whine.

"I just wanted to keep my baby! I thought maybe one good thing could come out of it, but she said I wasn't thinking clearly because Uncle Richie fucked my head up. She said he never loved me! She said all kinds of terrible things about him and I didn't know what to think. I didn't know what was real anymore....and it just kept going like that. She made the decision for me and I.... I don't know if I even know how to think anymore. I don't know if I even know how to love. How am I supposed to know if it's real? Maybe it's just the same thing and I wouldn't know it. My head is so fucked up that I'll probably never know. I'm too damaged, Wes! No one is ever going to love me and I don't know if I can ever love them. How can I know if I got it all so wrong? If I loved him, how can I ever know if loving someone is right? What if I get it wrong again?"

Now it all makes sense why she couldn't keep a boyfriend. Of course she couldn't. That bastard Uncle Richie really did a number on her head. Her father let him off way too easy.

I take a long time to decide what to say and I can't even be sure I'm glad she told me. Part of me wishes I didn't know. I feel poisoned by how bad it is. I want to puke, but nothing will ever get that poison out of me. I'm stuck with it forever.

I grip her hand tight. It's five minutes to ten—decision time. "Keep your baby, Natalie," I tell her. "This is your chance. You don't have to think anything. This is only for you. It's a gift you're giving yourself because you need this. You want it, so keep it. Love it and take care of it the way you want to. You don't have to make the right decision. Just make the one you want to make."

"But...." Her eyes swivel over to me for the first time. Thank God she's finally looking at me. "But.... what if.... what if this baby's father isn't going to be in its life, either? What if this is all wrong and I'm wrong for wanting to keep it? What if I do something terrible like make the kid live with something they can never get away from?"

"It isn't wrong. You don't have to wonder if you should love this baby. Just love it. Loving it can't be wrong."

"But what if.... what if I don't know how to?"

"You do know how to."

"How do you know?"

Her voice hurts, but I can't leave her alone in that place anymore. I reach out and touch her cheek. "You love me, don't you?"

Her face spasms in agony and her mouth goes all the wrong ways. She looks down at the floor. "I loved you so much! I loved you more than anything! I would do anything, Wes! I just don't know how...."

"You do know how and you did everything right. You love me and I love you. You love this baby and I love this baby. Nothing can ever be wrong with that."

She quakes with sobs, but I don't try to stop her or comfort her. It's 9:59. It looks like we aren't going anywhere.

She finally looks up through rivers of tears. "What do we do now?"

"Now I tell you something." I straighten up in my seat and stare through the front windshield. "Something I've never told anyone."

"What is it?"

"When I was a kid, I used to have these dreams about someone coming to get me. I used to see a man....and a woman....and kids playing in a field......And the man and the woman came to get me....... they were just out of town or something.... looking for me. They didn't know where I was, but they were looking for me and as soon as they found me, they would take me home.... home to that field with the kids playing and the man and the woman watching them."

I swallow hard. I have to tell her. I have to get this out before we go any further. I can't have her saying she loves me without her knowing.

"They didn't come. They didn't find me and they didn't take me home......but they were still there....in my mind......" I look over to find her wet eyes riveted to my face. "You were the woman. You were the one watching those kids play. You were the one searching who would take that child home."

I don't know what it means and I can't tell anymore if she does, but I said it. Now she knows.

She sits with her head bowed and tears running down her face. Then she nods and mumbles, "I understand."

I'm glad she does because I don't, but at least those words are out there. I don't want to know what it is she understands. It's ten minutes after ten and she doesn't say she wants to get out of the car.

For no particular reason, I start the engine and drive back across town. I park in front of her apartment building. She doesn't say anything for the whole trip or after I park.

I hold out my arms to her. "Come here, baby."

I pick her up out of her seat, turn her around, and sit her down on my lap with her legs curled up. I pull her head down on my shoulder and she huddles against me still crying, but I love that sound. It's the sound of the last walls coming down and now I can hold her the way I've always wanted to.

Chapter 25: Natalie

Wes swivels me off his lap and puts me down in the passenger seat of his car. He doesn't hesitate to look at me and his eyes spark with their old fire. "I need to ask you something, baby."

I gulp. "What?"

"How many bedrooms does your apartment have?"

"Um.... three."

"Do you like it there?"

I shrug. "It's as good a place as any."

"Which do you like better—my place or yours?"

"Um......I don't know. I guess.... I like yours because it's more comfortable. You have all your stuff there and.... your computers and everything."

He nods, but he doesn't look away. For no particular reason, he starts the motor again. I don't know what to think when he drives back across town to his apartment building.

He takes me upstairs and sits me on the couch in the living room. "I want you to stay here for a little while, baby."

"Why?" I hear how tiny my voice sounds.

"Because I don't think your apartment or mine is going to work and I want to find one that will work."

I gulp again. Work for what? I don't have to ask. I already know.

He stands up, squeezes my hand, and starts to walk away, but I grab him and hold him back. "Wes?"

"Yes, baby?"

He turns around and strokes my cheek and hair. He doesn't try to pull my hand out of his grasp. I have to gulp again when I look into his eyes staring down at me.

All at once, I can't stand it any longer. I throw my arms around his waist and croak into his big, strong stomach. "I'm scared, Wes."

His hand closes over my head and he presses me into him. "I'm scared, too, baby. I'm scared shitless, but we can be scared together."

He pries me off him, sits down on the coffee table, and cradles my swollen face in his hands. He gazes at me with so much obvious love that I can't deny the truth anymore. Telling him my secret made him love me more, not less. He loves me....and I love him. Maybe it's possible after all.

He pulls me into his lips and that kiss makes me start crying again. He feels so good. Being with him makes me want to hope for so many things. Is it even possible that I can have what I want? Is it even possible that I can keep my baby without the world coming to an end?

He wants me to, and if he's helping me, maybe it can work. I couldn't do it on my own, but man, it scares the crap out of me! I don't know if I can live with this level of fear.

I hang onto him for all I'm worth. I can't lose him. I can't do this alone. He's my only lifeline. I wrap my arms around him for the protection he gives me from the very possibilities I crave so much.

My tears sting his lips and he breaks off kissing me to put his arms around me. He pulls me into a hug that makes me cry so much harder. I can't stop. "I love you, Wes!" I sob into his ear. "I love you so much!"

"Baby!" he whispers in my ear. "I love you more than anything!"

"Don't leave me, Wes!" I wail. "Don't let me go through this alone!"

"Never, baby!" he whispers. "You're never gonna be alone again—not ever."

I break down sobbing on his shoulder. I want to believe that more than anything. I can believe it because he's the one saying it. I want to disappear in the vast size of his presence, his mountainous being. I want to get lost in there and become nothing but a part of him. I can believe I already am becoming that when he holds me like this.

He pushes me back and doesn't kiss me while he waits for me to stop crying. "I'm gonna go out for a while, baby. You stay here, okay?"

"Okay." I feel bruised and exhausted. I don't want to go anywhere or do anything, and since I'm now unemployed, I don't have to.

He goes into the bedroom and comes back with a blanket. He steers me down on the couch and covers me up. "Stay here," he says again and kisses me once. "I'll be back soon."

He leaves and I can finally settle down in the silence. I'm in his apartment. His case files and computers are right there in the next room. He has to come back here eventually. I'm safe here. I couldn't handle being alone in my apartment right now.

The fact that he knows this makes me love him even more. I snuggle down in the blanket and finally start to relax. I'm pregnant. I'm going to have a baby. I'm going to become a mother.

My life is going to change in ways I can't even imagine. I'm scared. Every part of me wants to hide from that fear. I want to do something to make my life go back to normal, but it's too late for that. I'm doing this. *We're* doing this. Wes and I are doing this together.

I can't remember where in the conversation we decided to do that, but it's happening.

I lie awake thinking about everything for hours and then I fall asleep. I wake up hungry and look around. I don't want to just help myself to Wes's food in case I eat something he doesn't want me to. If we're going to do this, I need to learn his diet so I don't mess things up for him.

I can't bring myself to get off this couch. I want to enjoy this silence for as long as it lasts before the mayhem starts.

I'm just putting my head down when the door opens and Wes comes back. "Are you okay, baby?" he asks. "Have you been lying there all day?"

"I fell asleep. Where have you been?"

"I was driving around outside of town and then I had a meeting. You haven't eaten anything. Come on. Let's go get some dinner and then we need to talk."

"What do we need to talk about?" I ask.

"Everything. Come on. I'm hungry."

He takes my hand and we go back downstairs to his car. He takes me out to a nice restaurant where he orders another steak. I'm beginning to see a pattern here.

"What did you want to talk about?" I ask him while we eat.

He doesn't answer for a second. "Are you okay with all this?"

I shrug. "I kinda have to be, don't I?"

"You don't have to do anything. If you aren't okay with it, tell me now."

I look away. "I'm okay with it."

"You might be okay with it, but you aren't ecstatically happy about it."

"I'm just.... scared.... about everything."

He takes my hand across the table. "Is that the only reason?"

I nod down at the tabletop and grip his hand tighter. I need to hold onto him so I don't start panicking. I don't want to start crying again, either. I've done enough of that today.

"Are you okay with it?" I ask.

"I'm fine with it."

"You're fine with it, but you aren't ecstatically happy about it," I counter.

He shrugs. "I'm just scared.... about everything."

I squeeze his hand again. I wish I could put my arms around him right now. He's the only place I have to hide from this storm.

We leave the restaurant and get back in his car, but he doesn't go back to his apartment. He gets on the parkway and drives out of town. I get an inkling of where we're going as soon as we leave the city behind.

My nerves prickle when he starts following the lake. The setting sun throws beautiful colors across the water and the hills turn black along the horizon. I've never seen anything so beautiful and serene.

He turns off into another driveway somewhere. Heavy tree branches arch overhead and form a long tunnel of foliage. It opens out at the end and Wes pulls his car up in front of a house miles from town.

"What is this place?" I ask.

"Come on out and take a look. Tell me what you think."

"I love it. It's stunning."

I peer through the windshield at a long, low, farmhouse that has definitely seen better days. A porch wraps around the front and the gabled roof hangs over dusty upstairs windows, but the whole place breathes with some kind of hidden presence that makes it feel alive. Woods and fields surround it and the lake stretches away into the distance behind the house.

Wes opens my door for me and pushes me toward the house. "Go take a look around and tell me if you love it on the inside as much as you do on the outside."

I walk up to the porch. It creaks when I put my weight on it and the door hinges screech when I go inside.

The inside looks just as abandoned as the outside, but the house feels sound and comfortable. It just needs a whole lot of cleaning and fixing up.

I wander through the rooms and come to the kitchen in the back. A large empty area adjacent to the kitchen shows where the kitchen table should be. The back doors open onto another porch overlooking wide fields leading down to the lake.

I step slowly onto the back porch and climb down the steps into the field. This is the place. This is where the man and the woman watched the kids playing. This is home—the home Wes wants me to take that lost child waiting to be found.

Tears sting my eyes looking out over the lake. What a beautiful home for a child this would be….and a home for the man and the woman. It's so perfect….so peaceful.

He comes up behind me and puts his arms around me. He holds me while we watch the colors fade from the lake's rippling surface. The colors go through so many magical, heavenly changes from pale blue to green to navy and purple.

The stars and moon reflect on the water and the wind whispers through the grass at my feet. I don't want to leave. I want to stand out here and watch all night.

He kisses the side of my head. He doesn't have to ask. We're there. We found it. There's just one thing missing—the children running around laughing and playing.

I can face it now. I don't feel scared about anything anymore. I can't feel scared standing here. That vision makes me so happy. I can't wait for it to come true. Everything standing between it and me is just part of the same happiness.

"Are you ready to go home?" he breathes in my ear.

I nod. I don't have to tell him that I'm already home. We still have some miles to cover before we get here, but we'll get here. I know that now.

I turn around, put my arms around him, and kiss him. "Thank you," I whisper.

"I love you," he whispers back. Those words mean so much more now. They mean he wants this vision with me.

He's the man and I'm the woman in the vision. We're going out into the world to search for our child, and when we find them, we'll bring them home. I can't wait for that day.

He takes my hand and leads me back to the car. It's getting dark and he switches on the headlights as we swivel out of the driveway. I don't even mind leaving. We have so much to do and I want to do it.

He pulls onto the long road back to town, but something is missing. I reach over and lift his hand off the steering wheel. I love that he wasn't even thinking about this. He needs me to invite him and that makes me love him so much more.

He glances over at me and then immediately faces front when I kiss his palm. I kiss the muscles along his thumb and then use my tongue to pull his middle finger into my mouth. I suck it feeling the rising wave of desire and arousal sweeping over me.

I feel him stiffen through his arm when I start to suck his finger. He wants this. He wants me. I know he does.

I tilt my seat back and a thrill of adrenaline goes through me when I let go of his arm. He keeps his finger in my mouth and his breath rasps through his teeth while I suck his finger. He feels so fucking good and I want him so bad. My body aches for him.

He slides his hand down my neck and squeezes my breasts through my shirt. I want so much more, but he doesn't unbutton my shirt. He crawls his hand down my stomach to my pants and fingers me through the fabric.

I moan and try to press his hand deeper into me, but he doesn't try to get inside my pants. He doesn't do anything more than that until we get back to his parking garage.

He kisses me in the garage for a while, but he doesn't escalate. Why is he holding back?

He gets out of the car and opens my door for me, but he doesn't do anything until we get all the way back upstairs. He takes me into his bedroom and we both take our clothes off. It's still early in the evening, but I don't want to be anywhere but in his bed.

We climb in on opposite sides and he switches off the light before we both come together in the warmth and the dark under his blankets. He pulls the covers over my shoulders and sighs in bliss when I put my arms around him.

I collapse in the beautiful safety of being with him. We're together. We're naked in his bed. We'll do it again and all the maddening passion of our first encounters will come back to life. It's inevitable, but for right now, I can just relax into his side with his arm around my shoulders. I can feel that everything's all right now simply because we're together.

Chapter 26: Wes

I walk into the Celestial Hotel lobby to find Mike Reed waiting for me. He nods and shakes my hand. "Morning."

"Morning. What's the word?"

"Not good. The head chef fucked up the supply order again and half the food has to be trashed. One of the guests found a used mop head discarded under his bed and the reservation system crashed this morning and wiped all our reservations for the next month. The IT guys over at Monarch are trying to recover the data, but it isn't looking good. We might be in trouble."

I'm just about to answer when loud voices draw my attention to the front desk. A young man in a suit leans across the counter bellowing at the clerk. "I made that reservation a month ago! I have the confirmation email right here on my phone! I don't care if your system went down! You have the email right in front of you! You can see I have a reservation! What is wrong with you?"

I go over to the clerk. "What's the problem? Give him his room."

"I can't!" the clerk croaks. "I'm locked out of the system. I can't even issue key cards to let guests into their rooms. The whole system is jammed."

"We're working on it as fast as we can, Sir," Mike Reed tells the guest.

The guy gasps in exasperation and seizes his suitcase which stands next to him. "I am never staying here again as long as I live. I'm going somewhere else and you can bet I'll be leaving a negative review on this place."

He storms out and the next guest approaches the counter. I can't stay here listening to the next catastrophe strike. It's going to be like this all morning until they unwind whatever is wrong with the system.

I head for the elevator, but I stop when I hear more yelling coming from the restaurant. I take a peek inside and see the head chef balling out one of the busboys between empty tables. It's nine o'clock in the morning. The restaurant should be full of guests eating breakfast, but it's totally empty.

"I don't care if it was your grandmother who knocked it over!" the head chef is saying. "We aren't running a charity here. That machine cost five thousand dollars. Who's going to pay for it—you?"

The busboy yanks the towel off his apron and throws it on the floor. "I don't care! Take it out of my pay. I don't care! I'm leaving. I quit. I don't need this shit."

He storms off and the head chef snatches up the towel before he throws it on the floor in a rage, too.

I turn back to the elevator, but I can't bring myself to go upstairs to see what kind of chaos is going on in the Triple Star executive suite.

The whole hotel pulsates with hostility and danger. It's a completely different world from the one I saw that first morning when I came to visit Natalie.

It must have been like this under Bill Simons.... except for one thing. Everyone working here is a Monarch employee. Most of them have been with Monarch for a long time. Are all our other hotels like this, too?

I'm standing here trying to make up my mind what to do when a dull thud shakes the building. "What was that?" I ask Mike Reed.

"Not sure." He gets a notification on his phone. "Oh, shit!"

"What's wrong?"

"Sam from Mechanical came over yesterday and said the laundry press wasn't set to the right temperature. He went downstairs this morning and tried to 'fix' it." He puts air quotes around his ears. "It looks like we should have trusted the Triple Star guys after all." He sticks his phone in his pocket. "I gotta go. Good luck upstairs."

He walks off and leaves me standing there by the elevator. I still can't force myself even to push the button. I don't want to know.

None of this should have happened. None of this *would* have happened if we did things Natalie's way. The maintenance guys would never set the laundry press to the wrong temperature under her. The IT guys would never let the system crash and wipe out a month's worth of reservations. They would all care too much to let any of this happen.

I make up my mind in a split second, go out to my car, and drive back to my office at Monarch. I get a notification an hour later from Richard Hurt calling me to the boardroom ASAP.

I walk in to find all the directors glaring at me. "What are you doing back here?" Richard demands. "You're supposed to be straightening out the disaster at the Celestial."

"That's exactly what I am doing." I go over to the presentation display screen and plug my thumb drive into it. "This is a spreadsheet of all the maintenance issues listed for the entire Triple Star hotel chain for the last year."

"Is this going somewhere, Wes?" Walter asks. "How does this get the chain back up and running?"

"As you can see, Triple Star had fewer maintenance issues, critical IT issues, and structural issues in the past five years than they've had in the two weeks since Monarch bought out the chain—and that's for the entire Triple Star organization across the whole country. The entire Triple Star chain had fewer issues than one single hotel has had under our management."

"What's your point?" Richard snaps. "I don't see anything here that tells us how to fix this."

"There's a very simple way to fix this and that's to bring in the one person who made it happen. Natalie Fahey ran Triple Star for years with fewer mechanical, maintenance, and IT issues than Monarch for every year of her tenure."

"Natalie Fahey doesn't work for Monarch anymore and Mike Reed is our COO," Walter points out. "She said when she quit that she didn't want to work for Monarch."

"She won't come back after what happened at Triple Star," another director adds. "She hates us now."

"She would come back if she knew we wanted her to convert Monarch to her way of doing things," I tell them. "She would be delighted if she knew we wanted to turn Triple Star back to the way it was."

"We couldn't convert *all* of Monarch to her way of doing things," Richard argues. "Monarch doesn't do things that way. Triple Star—maybe. We couldn't change Monarch to that. It wouldn't work."

"Why not?" I counter. "Her way is more profitable. She's proven that a million times. I think the time has come for us all to admit that her way is superior."

"I wouldn't go that far," Richard grumbles.

"Think about it," I go on. "All these problems that have been happening at the Celestial happened under Monarch's management with Monarch employees responsible for the screw-ups. We can't even blame the walk-out for this. Just face the fact. Our employees don't care about us. Whatever it is we've been promoting isn't compelling enough for them to care and really invest in our success. Natalie is the only one who can do that, and if we bring her back, she'll bring all the old Triple Star employees with her."

"That might work for Triple Star," Walter argues, "but how do you plan to get Monarch to change? Our employees aren't interested in all that touchy-feely family stuff."

"You might be surprised," I tell him. "I would be willing to bet based on what I saw this morning that they'd be a lot more agreeable than you think. Natalie told me that it was the Celestial employees themselves who got the rest of Triple Star on board. The employees in other hotels didn't believe she was sincere until the employees got word out that it was real. We could do the same thing here. We can get Triple Star back on board and then let it filter to the rest of Monarch."

Richard frowns and rubs his chin. "It might work."

"How are we going to get Natalie back?" Walter asks. "I happen to know that Dreamland Resorts just offered her an executive-level position. She won't come back, and even if we could convince her, we already have a full-stack executive committee. We couldn't demote Mike Reed and put her in his place, not when he's the one who's been keeping our heads above water during this disaster."

"I think I might know a way around that and I think I might know a way of convincing her. Let me talk to her and see what she says."

Richard sighs. "I don't hold out much hope for this plan, Wes. Natalie Fahey has been a thorn in our side since the Summit negotiations."

"We have nothing to lose at this point," I tell him. "Things can't possibly get any worse, and if we keep going the way we are, we won't have a chain at all. If we can't find a way to turn a profit with Triple Star, we'll lose all the funds you invested in taking over the chain in the first place and the loss could drag Monarch down, too."

Walter raises his hands. "You made your point, Wes. You talk to her. I really hope you convince her. I really do."

Chapter 27: Natalie

I pull open my bottom dresser drawer and lift out a sweater I haven't worn in at least seven years. I throw it on a pile of clothes by my bed and lift out the second one. I haven't worn that one in five years. Why have I been keeping all this stuff?

I scoop all the sweaters into a black plastic garbage bag and push the empty drawer back in before I open the next lowest drawer. I find a bunch of old family photo albums in there, and after flipping through a few pages, I grab a box and start packing them up.

The job of emptying out my apartment to move over to the lake house is going much quicker than I expected. I finish my dresser in no time, but when I start on my closet, I get a notification on my phone.

I sit down on the bed and crack open my laptop to go over the documentation from Dreamland Resorts. They sure are enthusiastic about getting me to take over for their outgoing COO.

I'm in the middle of scrolling through their company prospectus when I hear the apartment door open down in the living room.

"What are you doing back here?" I ask Wes when he walks in. "It's only eleven. You should still be at work."

"I am at work." He bounces on the bed behind me, puts his arms around me, and pulls me back to lean against him. "How's the Dreamland offer looking?"

"It's a very good offer."

He nuzzles closer to my ear. "But?"

"I'm reading a lot about providing excellent service to guests, setting industry standards, and building a global brand of quality and distinction. I don't see anything in here about their company culture or forming any connection with guests. It reads like a stockholder's information sheet."

"What would you say if I told you I knew about another job offer for you?"

"I'd say you had been smoking something while my back was turned. No one is going to make any offers to me after the way things went down at Monarch. It's Dreamland or bust for me.... unless I want to become a stay-at-home mom."

"Is that what you want?"

"I might if I didn't feel like I failed. I don't like walking out on my career on something less than my own terms. If I was at the top of my game and decided on my own that I wanted to quit to become a stay-at-home mom, it would be different."

"It turns out that I do have another offer."

"From who?"

"From Monarch."

I spring off him, spin around, and gasp. "Monarch! You're high!"

"The Board of Directors think so, too. They don't think I can convince you to come back, but I told them I could."

"Why? How? What's the point? Monarch is going down fast. Why would I want to have anything to do with it....and besides, Monarch already has a COO. Mike Reed is as good as Monarch can get. Besides, you and I couldn't be involved if I went back. We would be superior and subordinate again."

"I'm not offering for you to take over as COO. I have a different position in mind."

"You! You're making the offer?"

"I'm making it on behalf of Monarch since I'm the only one high enough to think this might actually work."

"Okay. What's the offer?"

"I want you to come on as an independent contractor. We wouldn't be superior and subordinate so there would be nothing stopping us from being involved with each other."

"What would I do as an independent contractor? Sorry, but I don't have any IT experience."

"But I bet you know people who do—people who are intimately familiar with all of Triple Star's systems and operations. I bet you know someone who can figure out how to fix a glitch that wiped a month's worth of reservations."

I stare at him for a second and then burst out laughing. "It sounds like you really need help."

"We do and no one knows better how to do it than your people. Come back as our new company relations consultant."

"Relations!" I snort again. "That's one way of putting it. Your company definitely needs lessons on that."

"I know we do. The Celestial is a mess. The Board of Directors is a bunch of cold-blooded snakes and the employees hate working for us. The guests are swearing they'll never come back. Half of our restaurant supply order is in the dumpster out back. Come on, Nat. We need you. This is your chance, not just to make Triple Star as good as it used to be, but to spread that culture to Monarch. Please. If you don't come back, I'm gonna have to quit, too, because I just can't stand it anymore.

I can't stand seeing how bad it is and how much worse it's going to get."

I blink at him. He's serious. He really means it.

My heart leaps when I think about getting Triple Star back to the way it was before. All those people will get their jobs back. We can rebuild our family culture, contact our guests and tell them we're back in business, and converting Monarch will be even better.

Then the doubts creep in. What if it doesn't work? What if the Board of Directors makes trouble for us and I wind up quitting again?

Wes wakes me up by laying his hand on my cheek. "Are you in there?"

His eyes bring me back to Earth. "Yeah. I'm in here."

"What do you think? The Dreamland offer doesn't start until the beginning of next year. At least try it. We can start your independent contract on a six-month trial basis. Mike Reed is on a six-month contract and that's when we're supposed to review Jules Hill's emergency leave. We can decide then who will work best as COO, and if you don't want to sign on as COO, you can just keep consulting independently."

"I won't be able to come on as COO—not if you and I are still together."

"We will be." He leans in and kisses me. "I promise we will be."

"Then I'll have to stay independent."

"Would that be so bad? You wouldn't have to worry about the operations. You could just concentrate on dealing with people which is your real superpower anyway."

"Okay. I'll do it."

"Great." He starts kissing me again, but when I try to pull him down on the bed, he resists. "I should go back to the office. I'm supposed to be at work right now and you have packing to do."

"Can't you stay just a little longer?" I wrap my arms around his neck and drag him down.

He sinks on top of me kissing me and rocking his body against me before he suddenly pulls off. "There. I stayed just a little longer. Now I gotta go."

"I'm gonna get you for that," I grumble.

He laughs on his way out of the room. "Call your people and tell them to come to the Celestial tomorrow morning at nine o'clock. We'll onboard everyone then and they can get straight back to work."

"Hey!" I call after him. "Were you serious about a glitch that wiped a month's worth of reservations?"

"You'll see when you get there!" he yells back and the apartment door slams shut.

I turn back to my computer where the Dreamland offer stares back at me from the screen. Am I really going to do this? Am I really going to get Triple Star back up and running?

That soaring feeling in my heart answers the question for me. I can't think of anywhere in the world I'd rather work, but if I'm actually doing that, I have some phone calls to make—a lot of phone calls.

Chapter 28: Wes

I have to work hard not to let nerves get the better of me while I sit in the Monarch boardroom waiting for Natalie to show up.

No one here seems too concerned about it—except for Mike Reed. He's the only one who realizes just how much our company is about to change. I'm not sure I can stand the anticipation.

The directors mill around chatting like this is just another day at the office. They have no idea what they're in for.

My phone buzzes in my pocket, but I don't take it out. It's my ten o'clock reminder—time for Natalie's first meeting as our new independent relations consultant.

I will myself to stay in my seat when the doors swing open right on the stroke of ten. She wears her best suit and she looks just as stunning and put-together as she did that very first day when I met her at the Summit Hotel.

She casts a flinty glance around the boardroom. She didn't leave here on the best of terms last time, but now she's holding all the cards. She knows we're sunk without her and she oozes confidence, but she doesn't lord it over us. She wouldn't do that.

The directors migrate to their chairs. "Thank you for coming in, Ms. Fahey," Walter begins. "We hope you can work this business out for us."

"Thank you for having me. I'm certain I can."

"So what did you want to talk to us about, Ms. Fahey?" Richard asks. "We understood that your new position as our relations consultant had to do with employee-guest interactions."

"A company's culture comes from the top," she tells him. "The Board of Directors and the executive committee set the tone and set an example for the rest of the company. If you don't treat each other like family, how can you expect anyone else to?"

"That isn't what we agreed to," Richard tells her. "There's nothing wrong with the Board of Directors or the executive."

"Really?" She pulls up a bunch of charts on the display screen. "This graph shows your employee retention numbers for the last fifteen years. You can see that the number has been dropping steadily for a long time. This graph shows your repeat guest numbers falling at an almost identical rate. This graph shows the number of employee resignations, either immediate walkouts or notices given, just in the last few weeks since you took over Triple Star. Resignations have skyrocketed across the entire Monarch chain, not just recent Triple Star acquisitions. That tells me that whatever personnel issues Monarch currently has were already entrenched in your company culture long before you ever took over Triple Star."

Dead silence falls over the boardroom except for a few nervous shuffles here and there. I struggle to keep still, but my heart won't stop racing. She's doing it. She's the best at this. She'll make them see the light. She's the only person who can.

She switches off the screen. "I want each of you to turn to the person next to you. I'm guessing you already know this person well. You've probably known each other for years. I want you to greet this person like they were your best friend or maybe even your sister or brother. Greet them as a member of your own family and talk to them the same way. Find out anything you don't know about them. See if they're having any problems. See if anything is bothering them—something you might be able to help them with. Maybe something is bothering you that they might be able to help you with." She waits, but no one moves. "Go on. Do it."

Another tense silence falls over the room and then we each turn to the person sitting next to us. I turn to the person next to me, which happens to be Mike Reed.

He gives me a wild grin, his cheeks flush, and his eyes flash with crazy lunatic excitement. He wasn't with me at the Summit negotiation, but he's been working side by side with Natalie since the takeover. He knows what Natalie is all about.

He sticks out his hand to me. "Good to meet you. I'm Mike."

I burst out laughing and shake his hand. "I'm Wes. How you doing? Do you have any problems I might be able to help you out with?"

"I think you just did." He shoots a smirk in Natalie's direction. She's busy hobnobbing with Walter. "She's a piece of work, isn't she?"

"She's the greatest. She's gonna give this company the shakeup it needs."

"How about you?" Mike asks. "How are you doing? You went through a rough patch there for a while, but you look all right now. Is there anything you need?"

"I'm good now." I let my eyes dart over to Natalie. "I have everything I need now."

He follows my gaze and his eyes widen. "No way."

Now it's my turn to smirk and my cheeks burn. "Yeah."

Mike bursts into crazy muffled laughter and presses his wrist to his mouth. "Holy shit! Congratulations!" He grabs my hand and pumps it. "I'm happy for you. You deserve it."

"Thanks, man." I can't help blushing. I've never been this happy in my life. "Hey, you want to know a secret?"

"What?"

"I'm gonna be a father."

His jaw drops and his eyes fall out of their sockets.

His reaction makes me blush even more. "Don't tell anyone. You're the only one who knows."

He gapes at me for a second and then shuts his mouth with difficulty. "Holy shit!" he whispers.

"Yeah! I don't know what to do with myself."

"You're gonna be great." He claps me hard on the shoulder and shakes me. "It's gonna be crazy at first, but you just gotta hold onto the seat of your pants and try to enjoy the ride. Holy shit—I can't believe it! You? I never would have guessed."

"Me, neither. I feel like I'm gonna explode."

He laughs again. "Yeah. It's like that."

"Okay!" Natalie calls out. "Let's take a minute to just let that sink in."

Everyone faces front and she goes on with her presentation. I cast one last glance over at Mike to find him grinning at me like a fool.

I've never felt this close to one of my employees—except for the night when Jules Hill quit. I feel closer to Mike Reed than I've ever felt to anyone besides Natalie. I actually feel like he might be a friend.... or a brother.

He's a father. He has a wife and three kids. He knows exactly what I'm going through. Whatever happens, I'll have at least one person in my life that I can talk to about this. This method of Natalie's really works.

I can't tell whether the Board of Directors feels the same way about talking to each other. Some of them look pretty pissed off about it. They look comical to me now.

She talks a little more about the benefits of this method and then she tells everyone to just mill around the room talking to each other. She gives them strict instructions not to talk about work. They're only allowed to talk about personal stuff and to treat each other as family.

I wind up talking to Jim Kaufman and two other executives, but they're so stiff and defensive about all this that I don't make any headway. That's okay. I got Mike. That's enough.

It started with the two of us. It will spread through the rest of the company. It's only a matter of time.

Chapter 29: Natalie

I show up at the Celestial Hotel early to check out how things are going before the big employee return, but when I get out of my car, I can't even get near the front entrance.

Dozens of people crowd the sidewalk and spill over into the driveway. The valets stand at the back of the mob and they keep casting backward glances over their shoulders, but no cars pull into the driveway. No guests arrive to check in.

Word has spread through the internet about how badly things are going at the Celestial since Monarch took over. The computer glitch that wiped all the reservations still hasn't been cleared up yet, so no one is checking in.

The Celestial should be a ghost hotel, but instead, all the old employees pack the lobby in droves. I can't get in until Tommy spots me. "Hey!" he yells over the crowd. "Natalie's here! Let her through! Hey! Make room for Natalie to get through!"

Word spreads through the assembled employees and they squash themselves to either side so I can wedge myself in. There still isn't enough room even with people trying to flatten themselves to the walls. People jostle and shove me until I get near the elevators.

Everyone is here from every department—maintenance, restaurant, cleaning, laundry, management, and even the executive.

More people take up the call as I get to the front. By the time I pass the front desk, the employees start chanting, "Nat! Nat! Nat! Nat! Nat!"

At long last, I reach the elevators to find Wes, Mike Reed, Jim Kaufman, and the other Monarch execs there. They must be trying to onboard these people, but no one can hear anything in the chaos.

Wes pulls me out of the crowd and yells in my ear. "You better talk to them! They won't go anywhere or do anything until you say something to them!"

I look around for somewhere I can address the crowd. Don't ask me what I'll say.

I climb up on the edge of a potted tree planter in the lobby. I wobble and almost fall before Mitch grabs me and steadies me.

Silence falls over the assembled employees once they see me there. Every eye turns up to stare at me. Now I really have to figure out what I'm going to say.

I clear my throat. "Um......thank you all for coming. As you know, I'm working for Monarch Resorts Group now as a relations consultant to convert Monarch to our family culture from the top down. We'll implement our family culture in all Monarch hotels, but we need to start that with Triple Star and that means you. You can all get back to work doing what you do best and treating each other and all our guests as family. As soon as the guests find out we're back at work, they'll come back and we can all go on as before."

Cheers rise out of the crowd and people take up the chant again, "Nat! Nat! Nat! Nat! Nat!"

I hold up my hands for quiet and I get it. I didn't let myself think I had this much influence over these people.

I clear my throat again. "The truth is.... I never could have done any of this without you. I'm just one person. You're the ones who did all this. You're the ones who accomplished all of Triple Star's success. You're the ones who treated our guests so well and you're the ones who gave all our hotels such a welcoming, comfortable, friendly, supportive atmosphere. You did all of that. I never could have done it alone and I love you all for that. I never wanted to work anywhere but with you, and if I can stand here today in front of you and say that Triple Star is the greatest place in the world to work and stay, it's thanks to you. You are the heart and soul of Triple Star and I couldn't be more grateful to be coming back to work with all of you."

More cheers electrify the crowd. People raise their fists and a surge of bodies pushes forward toward the elevators.

I really need to calm this down and tell everyone in the nicest possible way to get back to work, but I'm not sure anymore if there is any way to calm them down. The tide of noise and excitement out on the lobby floor escalates to a fevered pitch.

People smile and yell up at me, but I can't hear a thing. I glance over at Wes when a flash of movement catches my eye and makes me turn back.

A bunch of people still have their arms raised. They pump their fists in triumph, and at that moment, something else sticks out above their waving hands.

I have a split second to recognize the barrel of an automatic rifle before it explodes. It fires directly into the ceiling and people collapse screaming on the floor.

A single man remains standing in the center of the lobby. He fires dozens of shots into the ceiling and my blood runs cold when he swivels around to take aim at the crowd. He rotates in my direction and my eyes fall out of my head when I recognize Bill Simons. What the holy hell is he doing back here?

He glares at everyone as he wheels his gun from side to side. Screams and terrified shrieks erupt out of the crowd and people fall all over themselves trying to get away from the gunfire.

I stand frozen next to my tree. I can't stop staring at him. I haven't seen him in years and now he's coming out of the woodwork to wreak havoc on the Celestial Hotel and all its employees. How did he know we would all be here in one place at one time?

Deafening gunfire shatters my mind. I need to get out of the way. I'm the only person still upright enough for him to target and his eyes lock on me in deadly fury, but I can't move. I hold onto my tree in petrified shock.

He turns around and levels his gun at me when, out of nowhere, Wes collides with me, tackles me off the tree stand, and slams me down hard on the floor. He covers me with his body as bullets tear into the elevator wall right where I was just standing.

Ear-splitting crashes, screams, and booms pound the lobby above my head. I huddle under Wes's body for protection, but a second later, he grabs me and yanks me off the floor. "We gotta get out of here! Come on!"

He hauls me to my feet, and when I lose my footing, he tugs me to make sure I'm standing up.

He shoves me toward the hall leading to the bathrooms. There's an emergency exit down there, and with so many people packed into the lobby, the emergency exit is the only way out of the building.

He swivels in front of me to block me from seeing the mayhem unfolding in the lobby. Right before he moves into position, I catch one more glimpse of Bill rotating in a complete circle to target the other employees.

The employees nearest the front entrance scramble to their feet and stampede to get away from Bill's vengeance. The laundry guys are in the far rear and they hold onto each other to keep together in a group as Bill's rifle swings in their direction.

The gun stutters and my stomach plummets into my shoes as three bullet holes erupt out of Petey's chest. He topples against Rocker and Morland James.

"Petey—no!" I shriek and try to fight my way back into the lobby, but Wes won't let me.

He grabs me, wrestles me off my feet, and drags me kicking and screaming toward the hall. I can't think of anything but going back out there to help Petey. I can't let anything happen to him. I can't let any of these people get hurt because of me.

I'm so focused on Petey that I don't see Bill pivot around the other way. He turns in a complete circle and then his burning, hateful eyes migrate back to me. Flashes of fire belch from his gun barrel.

Some distant part of my brain hears the explosions of bullets striking the lobby walls. They get closer and closer as Bill brings his gun back toward the elevator. Those gunshots will strike the hall any second now.

Bill's eyes lock on me, and at the moment when his rifle would be aiming directly at me, Wes dodges in front of me and blocks me with his body. A bone-crushing impact strikes him in the back and hurls him against me.

He buckles and his weight bowls me off my feet before his bulk flattens me to the floor with him on top of me.

Chapter 30: Wes

I jolt awake and look all around me in a panic before I see that I'm in the hospital. Natalie sits on the edge of my bed looking down at me. "Oh, my God, baby!" I gasp. "Are you all right? Is the baby all right? Did you get hurt? Are you all right?"

She smiles down at me with tears in her eyes and lays her hand on my chest. "I'm fine and the baby is fine. You saved us. Everything's going to be okay."

I collapse back on the pillows. "Oh, thank God! I was so worried about you!"

She leans in and kisses me on the eyebrow. "You got shot in the back protecting us and you're only worried about us."

"Of course I am. You're everything to me—both of you."

She pets my cheeks. "I love you, Wes."

"I love you, too, baby. Come here. I need you here." I pull her down on my chest and she sinks against me. My God, she feels so good here!

I comb my fingers through her hair and kiss her on the head. I never want her to be anywhere else.

"How is everyone else?" I finally ask. "How bad was it?"

"It was pretty bad. A bunch of people are still in the hospital and Petey is still in ICU, but he's going to make it. There were no fatalities—except for Bill."

"What happened? I don't remember anything after I got shot."

She sits up to face me, but it's all okay, now that she's resting her hand on my chest and I can touch her as much as I want.

"The Police showed up not too long after you got shot. They killed Bill and then it was just a question of getting everyone to the hospital. I got stuck under you until they took you away, but I'm all right. I was just worried about you, obviously."

"I'm okay, baby," I tell her. "I just needed to know that you and the baby were all right."

"We are, thanks to you."

At that moment, the door opens and Logan Braithwaite comes in. He was CMO for Triple Star before the Monarch takeover.

He comes over to the bed and holds out a bunch of file folders to Natalie. "IT called, Nat. They got the glitch straightened out. The system is up and running again and our people are going through the bank records to find out who made reservations. We're contacting the guests to ask them to re-submit their requests so we have their stays on the system. Word is going out that Triple Star is back on deck and we need to...." He breaks off when he sees me awake. "Hey, man. You're back from the dead. That's excellent. It's good to see you back."

He sticks out his hand and shakes mine.

"Thanks, man," I reply and turn to Natalie. "Why are you handling the glitch? Is Mike Reed all right?"

"He quit," she tells me. "He got shot in the shoulder and he and his wife decided they needed to spend more time together as a family. He said he's been working way too much and he needs to power down so he has more time to concentrate on what's really important. Jules Hill quit, too, Wes."

"What? Why?"

"He isn't sure he wants to come back at the end of his leave and he doesn't want to take advantage of your generosity by drawing emergency pay if he doesn't plan to come back. Monarch wants me to take over as COO, but.... I'm still not sure if I should or if I should keep contracting independently."

I squeeze her hand. I want to do more, but I can't with Logan around. "Maybe there's a way you could be COO and still maintain your independence."

"How?" she asks.

"I mean maybe you could change your role as a contractor from a consultant to COO. I don't know. I guess we would have to look into it."

"You should maybe heal up and get out of the hospital before you start thinking about work." Logan squeezes my ankle before he turns away. "See you two around."

He walks out of the room and leaves me alone with Natalie. I turn back to feast my eyes on her and stop when I see the look in her eyes. "Does he know about us?"

"Everyone knows about us now. The cat is out of the bag after the shooting. Everyone thinks you're a hero.... because you are."

She leans in and kisses me for a long time and then she sinks down to rest her head on my chest. She lets out one of her long sighs of relief and her arms slip around my ribs.

She feels beyond good here like this. I want to ask so many questions, but mainly I just want to keep asking her every minute of the day if she and the baby are all right. My whole world hangs on them.

At least I won't have to explain to everyone why I care about her so much, but her explanation brings up even more questions. "Did you tell everyone about us?"

"I didn't have to," she mumbles into my chest. "I got kind of hysterical after you got shot. Everyone heard me crying and begging you not to die. Logan had to pull me away from the paramedics so they could work on you and then I kind of lost it when they took you away from me. I guess everyone kind of worked it out from that."

I press my nose and mouth to her hair trying desperately to hold back this tide of emotion. I love her beyond words and she loves me. She can't stand the thought of losing me and what we have.

Telling her I love her doesn't cover how I feel about her. I'll do anything to protect her and our baby. I'm the man that takes care of her. I'm the man she cries over and can't live without. I don't want to be anything else and now I never have to be.

The whole world knows about us, and as soon as I get out of here, we're going to make this real. Nothing will stop us as long as I have her here, right here in my arms where she belongs.

As soon as I get out of here, I'll take her home. She was lost, but I found her and I'll take her where she can be happy. She can rest there in the sunshine and I'll make sure she never gets lost again.

Epilogue: Wes

I slam my car door shut and gaze across the park to where a column of smoke comes from the barbecue on the other side of the field. I can't see who's doing the barbecuing, but it smells fantastic.

A bunch of guys from Triple Star are playing touch football out on the lawn with at least ten kids running around among the men. Andy Ireland breaks from the huddle and spots me walking into the park.

"Hey—Wes is open!" he yells. "Wes—go long!"

I run down the field and everyone comes after me in a pack. Andy sends the ball spiraling toward me and I catch it, but when I turn for the non-existent goalposts, I meet a wall of bodies of all sizes.

I dodge the first six or seven guys, shove Harvey Joiner out of the way, and make a break for the goal line when a whizzing comet of energy hurtles at me from the side.

I don't see it in time before my seven-year-old son Danny collides with my knees and drops me like a ton of bricks. I go down hard and then all the other guys pile on top of me.

I groan in pain until they peel themselves off me. "Jesus!" I gasp. "This is supposed to be *touch* football—keyword: touch—not tackle."

"Good catch, Dad," Danny tells me and holds out his hand to help pull me up.

"You guys play your games. I'm the CEO. I'm way too important for this."

They all laugh and Harvey rumples my hair. "You love it. Admit it. You've been dying to get out of that office of yours. You need to get knocked around some. It's good for your health."

"Keep telling yourself that. Oh, look. Here comes Nat. She'll save me from you barbarians."

The guys laugh again and I pull away. A toddler barely able to walk totters onto the lawn and my one-year-old daughter Edie raises her arms to me.

I pick her up, kiss her, and sit her on my hip as Natalie reaches us. She slips her arm behind my back and kisses me before we head off to the barbecue. "Is everything under control?" she asks me.

"Yep. All set. Now I can enjoy myself."

The crowd around the barbecue parts to let us in and Edie wriggles out of my arms. I put her down on the ground and she toddles over to the coolers where she can support herself.

Mike Reed comes over to me and hands me a bottle of water. "Let me guess. You're having steak."

"You better believe it." I shoot a critical glance at Petey standing behind the barbecue. "Does he know what he's doing?"

"He's great. He learns from the best."

"How's life at Dreamland Resorts?" I ask.

"It's busy, but we're bringing the chaos under control. We should be streamlined by the end of the year. I'm hopeful."

"You're the man." I clap him on the shoulder. "If anyone can do it, you can."

"I learn from the best, too." He shoots a glance at Natalie. "Did you get that thing you were talking about?"

"Yep. I got it."

We stop talking when she reaches my side. She's busy talking to Jules Hill's wife Sharon, who sits in a wheelchair by the picnic table where an umbrella can give her some shade.

Natalie slips her arm around my waist again and I hug her shoulders and kiss the side of her head. She's the reason everyone here considers me a part of their family and everyone here is a part of *our* family. I wouldn't be anywhere else.

"So what was the meeting about?" she asks me.

"You know we aren't supposed to talk about work at these things, baby," I tell her. "You're the one who made that rule."

"Okay," she replies. "I'll just wait until we get home and then I'll ask you there."

"She got you, man," Petey calls over from the barbecue. "Now we all know who wears the pants in the family."

"You wait 'til you get married and then come talk to me," I counter. "How's my steak coming along, anyway?"

Laughter breaks out and Phil Ames yells, "Don't mess up Wes's steak or all hell will break loose."

I turn back to Natalie. "Anyway, I wasn't in a meeting. I just had to pick up some paperwork."

"Oh. What about?"

I pull a folded sheaf of papers from my pocket and hand them to her. "Actually, it's your anniversary present. I wanted it to be a surprise. That's why I didn't tell you."

She stares at me and then down at the papers. Conversation dies and I become aware of Mike, Phil, Jules, Petey, and everyone else watching us. Mike elbows me when he sees her reaction. "I told you she'd love it!" he whispers in my ear.

"What is it?" she asks.

"Open it and find out." I hold out the papers, but she keeps eyeing them like they might be dangerous. "Don't worry. It's nothing bad. I did it for you.... for all of us."

She glances around at the faces smiling at her. Everyone knows but her. She's the last to find out.

She finally gulps, takes the papers out of my hand, opens them, and stares down at them. "What does this mean?"

"It means I bought out the last Monarch stock. I'm the sole owner and I'm taking the company private. It means no one can come along and change it to something we don't like without our permission."

She still doesn't respond, so I sidle over to her, put my arm around her, and draw her away from the crowd.

"I want you to become joint CEO with me. We're going to run this company the way it should be run and no one will be able to stop us. You won't have to contract independently anymore. It will be officially ours—all of ours."

She looks up at me with her eyes brimming with emotion. "Really?"

"Really. Tell me you're happy about this."

She winds her arms around my waist and buries her face in my chest, but she keeps her head turned away from the barbecue so no one can see her.

I have to hold her. I need her so much and now nothing can stop us from creating the vision that means so much to both of us.

The guys smirk at me from the barbecue. They know I've been planning this for a long time and I've trusted them to keep my secret. They're my closest friends—my brothers—my family.

Our kids play together out on the field. We share all the good times and all the bad times. We support each other in anything we need and now they're here to see me make this dream come true.

She leans back and rises on her tiptoes to kiss me. Her eyes give me all the answer I need. She's ecstatic about this.

It's the beginning and end of a dream that will just keep going. It will spread everywhere now that we have our people in businesses and companies all over the country. It will keep spreading until it transforms the world into this little paradise we've created in this park.

We turn back to the barbecue. Edie comes back over and Natalie picks her up. Danny yells and runs around on the lawn trying to tackle everyone. Our other kids are down at the water's edge throwing rocks or whatever.

Our kids will grow up like this and no one will ever be lost again. If anyone out there is lost or missing, we'll just keep searching until we find them and bring them home, too.

The End.

If you enjoyed this book, please consider leaving a review. You can also support me on Patreon at www.patreon.com/InvisiblePublishing.

Sign Up Once--Get all A.E. Moran's free books including brand new releases

When Doctor Lily Rice moves into a small mountain town to live in isolation away from the world, she sets off a chain of events no one could predict. Her arrival throws town doctor Parker Davis into turmoil. Is Lily trying to steal his patients and drive him out of practice.....or is there something much more sinister at work here?

The two get thrown together by circumstance and fate, only for secrets from both their pasts to threaten everything they've worked to build. Can two broken strangers find happiness through devastation before disaster tears them apart?

Sign up at www.authoraemoran.com to read it for free.

About AE Moran

A.E Moran is the contemporary romance pen name for Theo Mann.

I write 70 books per year—and yes, before you ask, all these books are my original creative work. Nothing written under my name is AI-generated or ghostwritten because I write better than AI and any ghostwriter out there.

People don't read fiction for entertainment or to escape from reality. People read fiction to see their humanity reflected in another person's character and story.

This is my promise to you. When you read my books, you'll see your own humanity reflected in the characters and stories. I take this commitment to my readers very seriously. My books are an intimate form of communication between us. I would never disrespect my readers by turning that over to a machine or another writer. This is my bond between me and you as my reader.

I write 20,000 words per day as my daily work output. If anyone with a public platform would like to challenge me to prove this in a controlled environment, feel free to contact me on this website's contact page. How do I do write so much? Find out more on my blog, *Crimes Against Fiction* at www.theomann.com.

I worked as a professional ghostwriter for fifteen years. Now I'm going for the Guinness World Record by writing 700 books over the next ten years and 1400 books over the next twenty years, all originally written by me.

See my website for the full book list. I'm also the author of *Proof for the Existence of God* and the *Crimes Against Fiction* blog.

You can find out more at www.theomann.com or at www.author aemoran.com.

Also by AE Moran (so far)

<u>Standalone Novels</u>

Heart on a Knife Edge

Dream Dimension

Just Friends

Back From the Dead

Damaged

Small Town Reunion

<u>Series</u>

Firehouse Blues (Books 1-10)

Turning Point Ranch (Books 1-10)

The Billionaires' Club (Books 1-10)

www.ingramcontent.com/pod-product-compliance
Lightning Source LLC
Chambersburg PA
CBHW070108030726
47506CB00002B/645